Advance Praise for *The Last Day of Paradise*

"Kiki Denis's debut is a slippery in-your-face accelerated rush of sex, hokum, and Greek family life. A little bit Eurydice, a little bit Chick-lit, with non-stop riffing on reality, time shifting, and the sheer punk roar of wordplay. She possesses the bent prowess of a metallic panther. I love the magic in her over the top writing."
—Richard Peabody, Judge for the contest and Editor of *Mondo Barbie*

"*The Last Day of Paradise* spins a tale of fateful passions that has the rough and tumble humanity of Greek myths. In the small village of Artemis, 15 year old Sunday's perfect world collapses when she discovers that her father may not be her real father. Sunday promptly embarks on a quest for the "whats & whys", and we follow her journey as she reconstructs the tumultuous events of her parents' courtship and the circumstances that produced her. *The Last Day of Paradise* is a complex, warm, vibrant novel, which seamlessly packs a rollicking family saga into the luminescence of a coming-of-age tale"—Vanessa Fabiano, Editor of *Shortcut* and author of *Fish in the Bowl*

"Kiki Denis has written an exposé of the lives and manners of an older generation of Greeks in a rural society marked by oppression and hypocrisy, as it is related by a group of dysfunctional young people, their children!...written in a fast-moving, mesmerizing style with a good dose of irony."— Orestes Varvitsiotes, author of *Ancient Greek Athletics: Myths, History and Culture.*

"Kiki Denis's novel is ambidextrous; a) comic & tragic; b) autochthon & international; c) light & heavy... Denis's words turn from ideas, to ideologies and ideals; Mediterranean pride-, honor-, shame-, blood-, kinship-, and gender- notions reveal. Language identifies not only with culture, but simultaneously transforms it to an emotional path. As Denis masquerades the meaning of her words, she turns them into weapons."
— Maria Hnaraki, Ph.D., Modern Greek Lecturer, Cornell University

"Kiki Denis uses a Greek speak that's alternately earthy, raunchy and cheeky to tell the story of two generations: one rooted in the old country, the other cruising into the modern day. The mother and daughter of *The Last Day of Paradise* have mega differences, but their super strength in the face of difficulty sheds light on what it means to accept tradition and what it means to reinvent one's identity. I particularly like the contemporary catchphrases that spice up the prose. Young people don't smoke Camels; they fume animals. They don't screw; they jump. Reading this novel is like watching *My Big Fat Greek Wedding* with commentary by Roseanne Barr."—Thaddeus Rutkowski, author of *Tetched* and *Roughhouse*

"*The Last Day of Paradise* is a novel with wit and attitude to spare. Kiki Denis's voice is as manic and moody as the Greek family she chronicles, and her debut is a captivating and wild-tongued tale."—Dean Bakopoulos, author of *Please Don't Come Back from the Moon*

The Last Day of Paradise

a Novel

by Kiki Denis

Arlington, Virginia

Copyright © 2006 by Kiki Denis.

All rights reserved under International and Pan-American Copyright Conventions. Printed in the United States of America.

With the exception of brief quotations in the body of critical articles or reviews, no part of this book may be reproduced or transmitted in any form or by any means, graphic, electronic, or mechanical, including photocopying, recording, taping, or by any information storage or retrieval system, without the permission in writing from the publisher.

Published by Gival Press, an imprint of Gival Press, LLC.

For information please write:
Gival Press, LLC, P. O. Box 3812, Arlington, VA 22203.
Website: www.givalpress.com
Email: givalpress@yahoo.com

First edition ISBN 1-928589-32-4 (ISBN 13: 978-1-928589-32-7)

Library of Congress Control Number: 2006924424

Bookcover artwork by Li Fan & Xu Yue.

Photo of Kiki Denis by Yiannis Tsiounis.

Format and design by Ken Schellenberg.

For
my baba who provided me with the confidence to stick to my beliefs,
my mama who kept me rooted to the great grounds of reality and
my brother who often forgets how cool he used to be and still is.

And of course mostly and lastly
for Yiannis, my joy in life.

The Great Entrance +
The Abrupt Interruption (1964-1980)

My name is Sunday. I am a person, not a day. Several months ago, I would have said I was an extra cool person with lots of self-confidence, but that was then and that's very far from now.

Anyway. Do you know that I have a friend who—just by looking at you—is able of telling you how many kilos of self-confidence or ambition you possess? Yes!!! It's true. Such a person exists. His name is Antonis and I haven't *jumped* him or going to 'cause real friends aren't for *jumping*, as people who possess more than ten kilos of common sense know.

How many kilos of common sense you've got?

Regardless of your answer I must add that Antonis is also capable of converting your kilos into pounds without using a calculator, or any other computational device for that matter. He could look at you and automatically be able to tell you how much self-confidence/ambition/common sense you possess and to what measure you have been trained to comprehend that amount. Of course he would say nothing. Why? 'Cause knowing that amount means knowing THE SELF, which might be a pretty scary thing, and Antonis doesn't like scaring people who don't know.

I wish I could introduce you to Antonis right away, but, first, I gotta talk about me, secondly about my happily brief past, thirdly about the ordinary day of the unordinary event, and then the present scatological situation.

7

So let's start from the start: me. I am a female with pretty boobs. (We'll get to the bs later on). I am also the only offspring of my parents, which makes me luckier, prettier, smarter and cooler than other offspring who have to share their prettiness, smartness and coolness with brothers and sisters. I was born to excel and raised to believe I could do so easily and smoothly.

My mama comes from a seriously loaded family, the Calliga family. My baba comes from exactly the opposite side. And because of this unfair distribution of wealth I grew up in a not-so loaded family, in other words, with micro-major economic problems. Of course that's my personal view of the matter 'cause mama still believes that money doesn't buy happiness only rents a portion of it and those who depend on rent end up homeless.

Anyway one thing is sure that my parents lacked desirable dough, and I said lacked and not lack 'cause currently there is much more around which is certainly a grand thing for me who I am an expert in maneuvering it successfully, endlessly and contentedly.

But before settling into the current situation I gotta give you a brief history from the early happy period of my life: the first fifteen years, eleven months, and seventeen days. So get ready. That was the time I had a pretty easy drachma-less life filled with respect, pride, family support and a dozen other things of the same category. I was living in an earthly version of paradise and on top of that entire domestic lottery I was granted an extra-cool yiayia, my baba's mama, officially known as Yiayia No. One. Note that baba's baba, my pappoo and famously known as my almost-full-time-drunk-pappoo, was in the great heavens, totally dead. My mama's parents were excused, they had announced their declaration of independence from being mama's parents the day after mama left the Mega Calliga Aristocratic Mansion, and when I arrived, about nine months later, they were already unpleasant history.

So those were the days that mama was an official poor but respectful mama and spent most of her daily hours working in the mini mega-store she owned which was named after her, Chrysa (also stands for gold in my premium tongue, Greek). Chrysa, the store, was most of the time packed with ladies. And Chrysa, my mama, was most of the time running around helping them. Each day of the week, except Sunday, one Chrysa was inside the other and kept busy and happy. Chrysa, the golden brick lady, was 5x6 (meters), dressed in her natural colors—golden walls, golden shelves and an oversized ancient golden register, which stood in its center like an aromatic daisy heart. She was in a great central location opposite the deli, next to the butcher's and only a few blocks from the village square. She might have been petite size-wise but she was crammed with all the necessities a female needs. A sample list of Chrysa's goodies would go like this: pins, knitting needles, embroidery hoops, scissors, thread, yarn, fabrics, zippers, buttons and beauty stuff like tiny extra-shiny gold and silver mirrors, nail polishes, hair conditioners, shampoos, soaps (aromatic but not too much), golden hair colors (mostly for women) and house ware stuff like plastic plates, forks, spoons, toilet paper, white napkins, and ladies' underwear and on and on and on ...

You get the idea, right?

Chrysa was mama's second child (after me of course). Mama loved Chrysa and took pretty good care of her. She wiped her floor every morning and every night, dusted her golden shelves on Mondays and Wednesdays, and rearranged her goodies at the end of each month. And Chrysa appreciated mama's love and concern. She was cozy, warm and amusing, filled with good karma, attracting all the ladies plus the virgins of the village, and, little by little, she managed to become every female's favorite place.

Ladies were paying visits to Chrysa even when they were not in a need to buy something. For a grasp of fresh air. To get away from evil mothers-in-law. To hear a verbal version of the daily gossip *Hello-Magazine*. To rinse off their boredom. Virgins also acknowledged Chrysa's virtues but the reasons for their visits were slightly different and basically two, in the following order: 1) the lingering walk from their houses through the square to their final destination plus the return ticket home and 2) the necessity to obtain the latest beauty materials and tips. Both reasons aimed at the same premium goal, a good future husband. One boosted their natural gifts. The other provided the time to show them off.

Year by year Chrysa's popularity was aiming at glorious big skies so Chrysa No. One, my mama, started to think that it was time to expand Chrysa No. Two, the store. A year later the thought became necessity. Chrysa No. Two was over packed, not a place to breathe, so the augmentation took place and proved to be a great success. Within a couple of weeks Chrysa No. Two gained a decent amount of length and extra kilos. In her new dimensions she looked serious. Classier. Like a respectable lady after giving birth to her first child. And as a lady of her status she had more needs so mama had to hire a couple of girls to keep her satisfied. The good news was that day-by-day our micro-major money problem was deteriorating and was slowing becoming a mini-micro major problem. The bad news was that mama was too busy being mama and wife at the same time.

So she started complaining and wanting baba to abandon his job and devote himself to the common family good. At the time baba was working as a barber and his monthly salary was about one tenth of Chrysa's weekly earnings so mama's proposition made sense. So soon enough Chrysa No. Two gained an extra official parent and I got more freedom to do whatever I was doing. In the first year things were rolling extra-cool, and although baba's conversational involvement dropped to sixty percent (he didn't find ladies' discussions so thrilling), he seemed pretty okay and was definitely more than okay when by the end of each day he pulled down Chrysa's heavy shades and concentrated on counting the many drachma bills which were accumulating inside the register. It was then that he verbalized about forty percent of his daily quota. About thirty five percent of that was numbers. The other five percent was a repetition of a bizarre sentence, which went like this: "better than the fucking great sin, better than the fucking great sin," accompanied with a quick rubbing of his hands.

In the mean time mama was stuffing herself with all kinds of chocolates, (I forgot to mention that she claimed that she had inherited from her middle dead sister a sweet tooth which within those months was transformed into sweet teeth) so she started expanding in all directions, becoming more and more. By the end of that year mama became a double-size mama with a triple size laugh (haaa!) and a syrupy vocabulary calling everybody honey, sweetie, sugar and so forth. So reasonably enough I started thinking that something mysterious was about to happen. After a lot of thinking I ended up with two sober contingencies: one good and one not-so-good. The not-so-good one was that my parents were in the process of manufacturing another offspring and were trying to sweeten me. The good one was that nothing was going on, we were just getting rid of our micro major money problem so things were becoming mellow. Because I couldn't make up my mind which one it was, (although I studied my baba's vocab very carefully and watched mama devour her hard-dark chunks of chocolate with great awe) and because I hate surprises, I finally got the guts and popped the question.

"So what's the occasion for the extra-honeys, sugars and syrups, Ma?"

Mama smiled, squeezed me with both hands into her two gigantic melons and said, "Nothing. We are just a happy, happy family, honey." And then she turned the other way and asked baba, "Right, sweetie?"

"But of course! A happy, happy family, sugar," baba agreed and I was two hundred percent sure that something was about to explode.

That was the last month of my brief carefree life. Twenty nine days later, on an ordinary chilly spring afternoon, baba entered Chrysa No. Two furiously. He traveled twice from the knitting needles to the zippers and from the zippers to the plastic plates, inhaling and exhaling fully and deeply then cut his spherical route abruptly and with jittery steps walked straight into mama who was standing next to the aromatic soaps, grasped her long black hair and yelled,

"She isn't mine. Is she?"

A piece of chocolate fell out of mama's mouth.

"Is she?" baba yelled once more, but mama wasn't able to answer. She just stared, mouth wide open, in full shock. An extra long minute of silence lingered heavily and then baba, without saying another word, exited Chrysa as furiously as he had entered her a couple of minutes earlier, went upstairs, (note that Chrysa was the first floor of our house), packed his things and headed straight to his mama's.

By now I am sure you got a feeling that the language I am using here is not my mother/first tongue. Of course don't take it literally; I don't possess a double tongue, or a second one. The way I like to think of it is like this: I got one tongue working double shifts, English being the night one, Greek the day. And as shifts go, the night one is calmer, cooler, looser, darker in nature. The day one is clean, precise, stirring, full-scale, simply premium. So 'cause of this overworking situation, I may often use your language irrationally, inappropriately, over-loosely, but please spare the sweat and try to comprehend that it's not in my nature but rather in my nurture. You might say then, if you want to state something of importance write it in premium and let an expert do the transformation, but I can assure you that in that set up I would be acting like a fucking lazy bum, working neither shift to their required capacity. In my opinion things should be written as they have been thought and happened, and if they have happened in a second hand/second tongue code then let them be in that code, don't manipulate them 'cause they end up loosing their magical nature and become too damn rational. And since "the roots of a language are irrational and of a magical nature" as mega-legend Borges proclaimed some time ago, that's the way I should keep them.

Of course there is a rational explanation of how things got to their irrational magical state and I am sorry to admit that the explanation is rather simple and dull but a hundred percent factual. And it goes like this: after the unordinary event (in short, baba's departure) life turned upside down. For all of us: Chrysa No. One & No. Two, baba, myself, grandparents etc. And when I say upside down I mean it. Life before was a normal battle between two fields: the enemies' and mine. The enemies' field included an almost silent baba plus an extra-sweet double-size relaxed mama. Mine included an extra-cool yiayia plus myself equipped with thirty nine kilos of self-confidence and six kilos of teenage logic. So the set-up was overall fair. Or at least predictable.

But life after became a civil war between the wicked and the good. The wicked were half the size of mama (after baba's exit mama developed an allergy for chocolate and dairy products so she lost a lot of weight) plus her evil pal, Yiayia No. Two (that's mama's mama, Mrs. Calliga) who appeared almost from nowhere. On the good side I was ALONE equipped with only six kilos of self-confidence (you'll see how I lost the other thirty three) and thirty nine kilos of teenage logic (you'll see that too). Yiayia No. One vanished, so things got pretty unfair. My enemies started speaking in secret code— I'll give a brief demo in a sec—therefore I was forced to invent my own lexicon. So after a lot of thinking and considering that mama's English consisted of three words (yes, no and candy), and Yiayia's No. Two of one (God), I started conversing in English.

At first sticking to the night shift was something like going to a defense mode, in order to protect myself and piss off the enemies, but later on it became a chic cult, granting me with a trendy pair of wings and an alluring cultivated attitude among ignorant classmates. It was like working in a nightclub and after many years of shitty dark slavery you're given the opportunity to become your own boss, harass your own slaves. So that's how I became a full time night shifter, exercising the limited English vocab I possessed and putting the premium Greek to a rest whenever possible. Of course this linguistic swap resulted in many other things: I had to reevaluate my group of friends, get rid of the non-English speakers and add some who possessed the knowledge, the sentiment and the determination to stick to the foreign vocab. Also I had to limit my conversations with mama, which was great from my side, but offered mama with plenty of room to carry out her long, toneless, and pointless monologues. Anyway that was what life after required me to do and I had no choice.

So, since you got the linguistic explanation, now I think is the time for a demonstration of the secret code. But before diving into it, it would be useful to provide a little overview of Yiayia's No. Two persona (Wicked Yiayia, her official name). So here it is. There are seventy four kilos of Wicked Yiayia, two thirds of those are accumulated on the lower part of the body, mainly on her butt, and the other third is evenly distributed between her mega hairdo, and her left double D tit (right tit is missing). Also, Wicked Yiayia possesses a high-pitched voice turned on all the way to maximum volume plus an over-extended forefinger that moves up and down when in converse-mode. Wicked Yiayia talks the same way she walks: no stops, pauses, gaps or going backward, just straight ahead. She only needs to sense a feeble signal of weakness and then she goes on and on and on, forever and ever. Last but not least, she is a mega believer in God, the Greek orthodox version, which she calls GG (Great God), one of her many abbreviations.

So here comes the demo.

It's 11 p.m. Last night. Four months and three days after baba's departure. I am almost ready to go to bed after a poor dinner (green peppers stuffed with rice) plus a horrible conversation, or rather monologue, demonstrated by mama who claimed to be in a fuming mood over my latest behavior (only she knows what she means), and the phone rings.

"Ringggg!!!! Riinnggggg!!!!! Riiinnnggggggggg!!!!!!!"

Mama to me, "Get it."

Me, "YOU get it. It's your ma anyway."

Note that after baba's exit, Wicked Yiayia calls the house at least twice per day, 'cause she "cares" as she declares, although she doesn't say what she cares for, anyway big discoveries are left for GG.

So mama sends me a half-open-eye look and goes to pick up the phone. As soon as the blah blah settles, I tiptoe to the other room and lift up the receiver with extra care with the purpose to provide you with an authentic demo and perhaps get an update on the enemies' latest actions.

"Told her?" Wicked Yiayia howls like someone is pointing a gun at her.

-Silence-

Mama isn't in a responding mood although Wicked Yiayia provides her with a micro-sec before continuing.

"No? Why? GG! (Well that's easy, Great God.) When will you? Our FN (that's Family Name) is on the line here. You gotta get her to the DH (sorry, cannot decrypt this one)," Wicked Yiayia's voice sliding angrily through the telephone line.

-Silence again-

"Say something, d!!!" (D usually stands for damn it).

"Okay, ma. I am waiting for the right moment. Don't forget that sheee, she is … just a kid. You knooowww," mama responds, dragging her words more than usually in low volume.

"You gotta do it by the end of this week, you know that only by doing it you'll clear up the mud he placed on your face and our entire FN that b" (b stands for bastard here which stands for baba). "The p!"

(P is for pauper). "The DD!" (Dirty Devil) "The ff!" (Most probably she means fucking fool). "The..."

"Enough ma. Enough. He is my husband, my daughter's father. Don't ever forget that."

"I didn't ha." (Honey). "But HE, HE seems to forget it. Going around, spreading his nonsense and all."

And then mama's heavy breathing strives through the line creating a very distinctive noise. A bunch of long continuous exhales that go like this:

"Huuuuuuu!!!!!!!!Huuuuuuu!!!!!!!!Huuuuuuu!!!!!"

Yiayia continues, "Anyway, how is it with her?" (That's me.) "Did she stop that b (bullshit, really means the English) talk of hers? Did you manage to get an o (most probably stands for "order") in that b (big, broken, bullshit or something like that) house of yours? I told you one zero zero zero times (she does that with numbers, spelling them out one by one), you gotta time her, choke her ill habits 'cause she'll end up being like you know who." (She means baba.)

So at this moment mama takes an active role and finishes the conversation. "Okay ma. Hmm. Right. Right. Night. Okay. Goodnight now."

And finally Wicked Yiayia ends with her famous slogan, "GG (Great God) with you tonight and BD (Bloody Devil) with the enemies." (That's baba and his mama). "Goodnight ha, sd, sd." (Sweet dreams).

End of demo.

Based on mama's interpretation Wicked Yiayia is the biggest abbreviator of all time. Based on my observations Wicked Yiayia converses in secret code only with mama and when I am around. So go figure. It's fb (fucking bullshit), simply fb, I think and retire to my room trying to figure out what dh stands for.

The Bloody Next Day

It's 7:39 a.m. Mama enters my room and executes her evil morning act: slams the windows wide open with the excuse of letting *a glorious blur of fresh air into my dim, over-humid room.* In reality, trying to make my life as hellish as hers.

"Good morning honey. It's time. Get up. It's a beautiful, beautiful day."

Just from her sweet vocab and the double word-usage, I know that something unpleasant is about to occur.

"Come on sweetie. Get up. Honey? Sugar?"

The only thing I dare to put into my mouth during the weekly barbaric premature hours of the morning is a cup of black coffee with absolutely no sugar, so it's blindly obvious that all those verbal sweeteners over-upset my stomach and boost my bad mood and although mama is aware of it, she seems not to give a fuck. So I get out of bed with a stomachache and head for the bathroom hoping for a minute of double p (peace and piss), but of course mama follows.

"So! Honey! Sweetie!" A hesitating tone in her voice conquers her determined walk and makes me even more curious about the weird shit in progress. "So. Since there is no school today, I thought that it would be good if you come with me to the clinic. I am going for my annual check up, you know and…"

"What for?"

"Well, you are a woman now and…"

Wow!! That's a big discovery, I think, but I say nothing 'cause I don't want to enhance the enemy's attitude.

"So as a woman, having your period and everything, you can…"

What does she really mean with that everything? I wonder, so I decide to elaborate and spice up her mood.

"Are you referring to my mega sexual active life, Ma?" I ask yawning.

"Honey! Come on. You are a nice girl." She really means virgin but I banned the use of the word a long time ago 'cause it doesn't reflect the facts (although mama denies tenaciously to acknowledge that) and it's a bloody humiliating word.

"I just thought that it would be good to come and have some tests done."

"I think I'll pass, Ma," I declare and lock the door behind me.

"Sweetie it's not a matter of passing. You have to have those tests done. It's for your own good. It's…" I hear her mumbling outside the door and I dangerously develop an annoying mood.

So I yell, "Ma, my sex-life is great. Need no tests to prove it. And if you want to know something else, it's ss, safely sexy, as your mama would say. Durex extra thin with a strawberry bubble taste. So nothing to worry about."

"Honey, stop that nonsense. You know that when a woman has her monthly stuff she should go for pap tests. It's almost two years now that you are a woman and... and I thought..."

"Ma, I am not into it. You go and leave me out of it. Let me enjoy my f's."

I really wanna say it aloud but dared not 'cause I know that mama can't handle f words coming from my mouth.

"Honey? Sugar? What's all this talk? You know how I feel about all these things; I just don't want to be like my mama. She didn't even have the decency to tell us about all that stuff and we almost freaked out when we got *it* for the first time. You know how I feel, we are civilized people, we live in modern times, we have to talk like daughter and mother."

She means she talks and I listen.

"Honey? Are you listening?"

"Yep! I am all ears and, Ma, you are disturbing my creativity."

"Okay sugar. Finish doing whatever you are doing. We'll talk over breakfast."

Meaning the torture will go on.

So I dwell about an hour on top of the toilet trying to get rid of anal and mental waste and find a defense plan to prevail the gynecological examination. At about nine o'clock I retire, heading to the kitchen for the continuation of the torture scene episode No. Two and surprisingly enough I find mama waiting for me over a first class breakfast: eggs, toast with honey, freshly squeezed orange juice and coffee. It's the first time after baba's departure that mama has gone to all this cooking trouble and I am seriously worried to hear what she has in mind.

"What's the occasion?" I dare ask hoping for GG's mercy although I am not convinced about his magical powers or his existence for that matter.

"Nothing. I just thought that it's time to have a nice proper breakfast with my daughter. We haven't done it for so long, honey. Don't you think we deserve it now and then? Ehh? Don't you?"

I send her a suspicious look and decide to go into aloof mode (replacing my thoughts, actions and vocab with a dull, vague nodding). Mama senses it and goes on with her verbal act.

"So, how is it? The eggs okay?"

I nod, nod. What else could I do?

"As I was saying, it's time for you to go to see Doctor Katina. Have a pap test done. You know how many women develop a thousand evil things that they can avoid if they just keep up with the annual female routines? And these are young, young women, children like you. You don't have to be married to get the devil's thing, you know? It's not that I want to scare you or anything but we have to be realistic here."

As I am about to finish the eggs and continue with the toast, thinking that Katina is a prehistoric ridiculous name for a woman in general and even more for a gynecologist of our times, so at least if I am to exhibit my privates in front of someone I should be a bit fussier and choose a doc with a contemporary respectable name and not some ancient midwife who is accustomed to dive her whole hand inside overused abysses.

"One visit to the damn hospital will not hurt, baby. Will not hurt."

And all of a sudden it hits me. Damn hospital. DH. DH. So that's what Wicked Yiayia was talking about last night, I think and swallow a piece of my toast.

"Finish up, baby. We should be there by ten. I've made up an appointment for you and since you are going you should get a blood test done, too. You know, just to be on the safe side."

I hear mama going on. I pause, adjust my aloof mode, and say, "Cut the shit, Ma. What's up? What are these bloody tests for?"

My investigative look (eyes wide open nailed on the enemy) is on and she knows it. So she comes around the table attempting to squeeze my arm or something but thank God I manage to escape on time. Once more she places her half size butt on the chair, comes closer to me, wears her sweetest face and starts, "You have to do it for me, babe."

"But what's the reason? I have to know the real reason if I am to give my blood away, right?"

"I told you. And you don't believe me then what can I..." she mumbles determined to go on with her fairytale.

So I stand up, salute her with my right hand, say "ciao" and exit the scene with style.

I get out heading for Loo's thinking that the only thing I need is a Camel. *A Camel before and a Camel after is a must,* I recall George's words and smile. I pray George is at Loo's 'cause without his presence there are no Camels before, after or during.

GG hears my prayers so when I arrive at Loo's I find them all there, sitting in a circle, smoking their *animals*, listening to Maria. I hurry, take my post, start creating my own smoky rings.

"She had to take it out. You know, cut the genesis process in the middle, 'cause her *jumper* wasn't willing to take responsibility for the baby. So that was the end of her love story," Maria says between deep drags.

"Whom is she talking about?" I whisper to Antonis who sits next to me, eyes closed, smoking something more than a Camel.

"Someone who did it without the proper protection and ended up bloating in no time. Not important. She just talks. No real stuff. You know, hypothetical bullshit. You want my CAMEL?" he asks with a cunning look.

I shake my head no and recline into my seat. I try to replay the mama-episode in my head with the hope to uncover the bloody mystery. But I come up with nothing.

"Tell us about Puta's son, Stelio, and the beds," Maria says.

I put out my Camel, pause for a minute, and then start.

"So last week I was passing with Stelio by the mega-villa, you know the one next to the sea who belongs to the French chicks. I was going to my ma's old lady and he was going to see his godfather who lives further down on the same street. So as we are walking Stelio stops and looks at the villa and tells me, '*You know what I would do if I had this mega-extra deluxe villa for myself?*'"

I pretend to think for a sec and then I say, "I am afraid no. I have no fucking idea. What would you do?"

"I would take out all the furniture. All! Strip the whole damn house down and then go and buy about twenty mega-huge beds," Stelio says.

"Why so many?" I ask.

"Two for each room," he replies.

"Why two?"

"On one I'll be *jumping* you day and night and on the other I'll be jumping for joy," he says smiling and scratching his crotch.

And they all laugh. Antonis puts his CAMEL on my lips. I recline, taking a deep drag and swearing to GG that I will not open my legs or give my blood away without making mama spell out all her whats and whys.

Ancient Era

The Mega Kiss (Sunday September 1, 1963)

Before Great God's transformation to his present state of Greatness, he was simple God, and although he lacked his two capital G's, which he got unexpectedly in another pretty ordinary day, the Calliga family used to visit his modest house one day per week, and that day was Sunday. At the time God's house was a pretty small orthodox church about four blocks from the Calliga Aristocratic Mansion, which was the largest and prettiest house in the town of Artemis, located approximately ten kilometers west of Mount Olympus. So every Sunday morning the Calliga family took no breakfast in the living room like the other days of the week but got into their crystal clean clothes and gathered outside the main yard waiting for the Master of the house to make his exit from the bathroom. Master Calliga, who less than a year later was to be my pappoo, did everything in a hurry except one thing: shitting. That he did in a great slow motion, believing that it was the only pleasurable right to a man regardless of race or social class. It was proven that in that spacious white marbled room the great Master had come up with many innovative ideas about improving his family farm business, a thing that encouraged him to view his time there as a creative and (by all means) sacred era; therefore, almost no one was entitled to interrupt him. In other words, a shit for Master Calliga wasn't just a shit. It was more like a mega road to mental creation. So the morning of September 1, 1963, while Master Calliga was enjoying his last glorious peaceful shit, his youngest daughter, Chrysa, my mama to be, knocked on the door.

"Baba it's late, we have to get going. What happened? Did you fall in or something?"

It wasn't coincidence that my future mama was the only person who possessed the guts to interrupt Master Calliga's artistic moments. Mama was known for her wild, misbehaved personality but also known for her joyfulness, courage and honesty, characteristics she inherited from her baba. She was the closest copy of his majesty, personality wise, and he was pretty fond of her.

"Shit!" the Master mumbled, searching with his left hand for his gold pocket watch while with his right wiping any last scatological evidence.

"It's shit alright," his youngest giggled and exited the house.

Two minutes later the Calliga family was on its way to the church. First the Master with the Missus walking arm-in-arm, behind them the great and only son of the family, George (sixteen), and last and prettiest the three sisters: Zoë (twenty-three), Sunday (twenty) and Chrysa (seventeen). The truth was that Master Calliga had little respect for God and thought of Sunday mass as a waste of time, but for his Missus God was like a famous friend with whom you wanted to be seen so Sunday mass was a must.

About ten minutes later, the Calliga family made its stylish entrance into the crowded room and took its usual first-class seats next to the mayor. The priest started singing his popular songs with more than usual enthusiasm and the show rolled like every other Sunday. An hour later when the believers were asked to prove their faith, Mrs. Calliga took out of her purse an ironed bill of respectable amount and ostentatiously placed it on top of the sacred tray. Immediately afterwards she whispered into her husband's ear who was almost asleep that the first act was over and slowly they started walking towards the exit with final destination being the front yard where the most fun part was about to take place. Needless to say, the sisters followed, keeping previous walking arrangements. The dearest son of the family stayed in; his Sunday school was about to start and he rushed to get a front seat with the rest of the boys of his age.

The yard was in full bloom, numerous kinds of flowers: wild roses, lilies, chrysanthemums, geraniums, jasmines, etc. The cool north wind was almost magical so everybody's mood was in its peak. Nothing seemed to remind the believers that winter was on its way. As they stood there in the middle of the yard, class by class chatting and discussing winter plans, it felt more like the beginning of spring.

In that holy pleasant weatherly blossom Mrs. Calliga learned that so and so was to be married, so and so to have a baby and so and so to send his kids to the capital. The Master after hearing bits of the above conversation, got bored to death, so he walked over to the mayor's side and started spreading his philosophical ideas about education, taxes, employment and whatever he thought was on its way to hell under the current government. It must be noted here that Master Calliga was a very big fan of the royal family and had no tolerance for liberals, Marxists or democrats, whom he thought of sharing the same political ideas but using a different name with the only purpose to confuse the uneducated crowds. The Master was proud enough to have met the royals some years ago and, when possible, made a point of describing in great detail the whole incident. So as he was about to give a full report of the event for the hundredth time to the mayor, he realized he felt a gaping hole in his stomach and decided to drop the subject and cut the chase for a well-cooked delicious Sunday meal. With an agonizing glance, he signaled his wife. It was then that Mrs. Calliga, trying to gather her daughters, unhappily realized that her youngest was nowhere to be found. After a thorough but unsuccessful eye-examination through the crowd, Mrs. Calliga grabbed Sunday's arm and, giving it a harsh squeeze, asked, "Where is she?"

"Don't know," Sunday replied avoiding her mama's furious glance.

"Behind. With the boys," Zoë said proudly as if she'd just accomplished something, which deserved great recognition.

Mrs. Calliga took a deep breath, sent a quick but meaningful look to her husband and headed for the back. There she witnessed the most dishonorable scene for a lady of her status: her youngest tightly squeezed in the arms of a pauper (the young man wasn't wearing a suit or anything like that, just a cotton striped blue pair of pants and a matching semi-ironed short sleeve shirt) whom at first Mrs. Calliga failed to recognize, perhaps because of her state of furiousness or just because his face was too close to her daughter's so she didn't have a full view. The sinners seemed to be in deep erotic daydreaming when Mrs. Calliga grabbed her daughter's hair and gave an unexpectedly strong push to the pauper who landed on the holy dirt, mouth half-open. The rest is easily imagined. The youngest was dragged home without much talk but as soon as the family reached the main living room the mother ordered the rest of the members to go to the kitchen, then she sat the daughter in the middle of the room and started with three slaps that landed on the daughter's pinkish cheeks almost from nowhere.

"Mama, I did nothing," the youngest yelled a couple of times, but mama was too involved in slapping and talking.

"You will not shame our name lb," (little bitch) she yelled between short breaths. Then, "In God's house! Stupid!"

"Shut up!!"

"With the first pauper you find in front of you? Ls!" (Little shit)

"Shutt!!"

"I did nothing. I was just looking for Nikolas. Uncle Socrates sent me there. I did nothing. I did nothing," the youngest gasped while mega tears were cooling down her feverish cheeks.

"Shutt!!"

Based on six different independent sources the youngest wasn't lying, but her mama wasn't about to be convinced since she'd witnessed another version of the truth with her own eyes, so she gave her daughter what she deserved and when she got tired and hungry she locked her in her room and went to wash her hands. In the meantime Mrs. Calliga gave a slightly different version of the story to her husband because she knew that the Master wasn't very good in handling the whole truth. Without knowing the full details of that version, I imagine that something like this was said to the Master: *I caught your daughter talking to some man or I caught your daughter in the middle of the boys-crowd.*

Anyway, the told version of the story was enough to make the Master furious. Immediately after dinner he walked into his daughter's room, pulled off his leather belt and as he was about to teach his daughter what it meant to be a member of the Calliga family, his wife entered the room.

"Enough! Enough!" she yelled jumping between father and daughter, "I gave her a couple."

Of course the poor daughter knew pretty well that there were more than a couple.

"It's enough for now. Don't mark her. We won't be able to get rid of her."

That last comment stopped the Master, who by then had managed to slam his belt several times into the moist air.

"Bitch!" he shouted and exited the room.

"You are lucky lb, that he doesn't know the whole truth," Missus hissed into her daughter's face and then, "Ftoo! Ftoo!" she spat and slammed the door behind her.

It was that very moment that Chrysa dropped onto her bed, covered her face with her hands and started releasing her mega tears. And for the next couple of hours things were monotonously wet, going like sniff, sniff, and sniff, sniff and sniff sniff...

Pauper-The Mega Hero

The unidentified pauper wasn't really a pauper or, better said, he didn't think of himself as being one. He had a house which really was his mama's and baba's, only one room where the family did everything a family does in its house; sleep, eat, drink, talk, dream, argue, fuck et cetera, et cetera. Size-wise his single-room house was one eighteenth of the Calliga's Aristocratic Mansion, which had eight more double-size rooms plus a separate three-room servants' house which was currently empty, plus a yard about three times the size of the whole mansion, plus the stables area which accounted more than five times the mansion, so, in simple words, half the village. But let's leave geography aside for the moment and continue with the pauper. The pauper had a good looking round-shaped mama who liked women in all shapes and men only in one (strongly built upper body, thick black mustache, bright wide smile showing at least three white-teeth, a constant deserved-earned sweat and mega-heavy balls), an almost-full-time-drunk baba who had none of the characteristics in the latest parenthesis, an older sister in America, Olga, otherwise known as the Queen of Femininity, whom he hadn't seen for more than a decade and an almost educated younger brother, the Aromatist, who had a briefcase glued to his left hand and who went around talking about herbology and its benefits to raising good/honest citizens. The pauper himself also had a dozen things to be proud off: huge blue eyes; golden super-straight hair; a well built body; an anxious or cunning gaze, depending upon who or what was looking at him; pretty long fingers he was currently using with great skill at Gregory's barber shop; a broad vocabulary (including words such as lady, dearest, beloved, precious darling and fucking blue balls, fucking white balls, fucking gray balls, fucking shitty balls which could be easily translated to fucking yellowish-brown balls, the worst you can get color-wise); a strong faith in an unnamed great creator with a big belly and long white beard; a diploma from elementary school (GPA 5.5 on a scale of ten); 1,263 drachmas in the bank; a fake American gold watch from his sister; a black suit he wore on Christmas, Easter and the Virgin Mary's day, August 15th; five volumes of the *Britannica Encyclopedia* (year of publication 1951); and a loving heart about to be broken in a thousand pieces. At the time our hero was twenty seven years old, making just enough money to visit the widow's house at least once a week, a habit which most young men of his age possessed and declared as *the great fucking sin*. (Used as: Have you done *the great fucking sin* yet? Or: I am out of my pants man, gotta do *the great fucking sin*. Or: Please man, show me some modesty here I am in big trouble, lacking dough for *the great fucking sin*. Or: Ohhh! Man, you are out of equilibrium. Need to do *the great fucking sin*. —Get the idea?)

So overall the pauper was a handsome young man and would have been a pretty good catch for the ladies of his division if his baba hadn't had the habit of getting totally wasted, covering himself in his own vomit and shit and had to be dragged out of the same dry gutter by his family at least once a week. Of course, the poor drunkard without even intending had taught his son a lesson: booze (which in his case was ouzo) is evil. Stay away from it. Thus the son ended up hating any kind of alcohol and most specifically ouzo so much that he hasn't even tried it once. At least till then. Just imagine what kind of mule he was to be a Greek and never taste his national nectar. Anyway, the pauper ended up being a mega-anti-alcoholic dude possessing super dreams for himself: get married, build at least a three room-house with a backyard, fill it with kids and live happily ever after. And he wasn't only dreaming about those things, he was pretty determined to make his dreams come true. Of course, he wasn't aware that determination alone doesn't overcome fate, even if you happen to have more than your kilos. So although he possessed twenty dozen kilos of determination (in simple numbers two hundred and forty kilos) which was much more than his actual weight, he was totally unprepared, still in his yellowish underwear, when fate knocked on his door one humid August morning in 1963.

It went like this.

"Knock! Knock!"

"Fucking blue balls!!!" the pauper murmured while trying to get into his pair of pants.

"Who is there?"

"Knock! Knock!"

"Who the fuck is there?"

"Knock! Knock!"

"Don't you have a fucking name or something?" he yelled, opening the door.

And there before him was his old pal Dimitris or the impromptu poet as the pauper liked to call him, referring to his prime hobby which was writing songs on toilet papers, on the back sides of cigarette boxes, and in his mini black leathered notebook that he carried with him day and night. It must be said that Dimitris, the impromptu poet, was good at writing. On paper he was a different man. Smooth, suave, soft, silky, sugary, sweet, syrupy and all the other s-words with analogous meanings (shitty-not included). So Dimitris was the king of paper but just another fucking fuck verbally. In simple language, he sucked.

So the pauper took a good look at Dimitris, slammed the door behind him and asked, "What's up man? Why the fuck don't you answer? Did you swallow your tongue or something?"

No, Dimitris hadn't swallowed his tongue, the widow swallowed his big fucking tsootsoo the previous night but his tongue had nothing to do with it; it was definitely secured in its place. He was just in such excitement that he had no breath for words. You see the previous night he was at Paradise (the local tavern) and there he got into this mega argument with Fucking Auntie Puta, who wasn't really his auntie but a freaking over-suppressed huge hairy *sister*. Let's point out here that *sister* in Greek is not the equivalent to the Negro's slang *brother* or *buddy*, in Greek *sister* is homo, gay, or the fake lady who possesses a pair of defective balls. So Fucking Auntie Puta, who was also famous for his mega bitch tits and for doing it with all the loose-leash animals in the village, including the widow who demanded triple her normal dues with the excuse that she had to waste at least a dozen cucumbers to cool down his thirst, was trying to convince Dimitris that he was a bloody loser 'cause he was about to reach his thirties and the only woman with whom he had done it was the overused widow. Furthermore Fucking Auntie Puta was telling Dimitris, and, of course, the rest of the tavern was all ears, that he wasn't just a fucking loser, he was also a pervert, a dirty scam with an Oedipus complex and that's the reason he was doing it all those years only with the widow and hadn't even gotten close to the fresh flesh of a young virgin chick. Of course, Fucking Auntie Puta's words had a spice of truth but they lacked the details of an herbal recipe. Dimitris hadn't gotten to the virgin chicks yet because he hadn't reached the searching state for his future wife, which, based on his standards, was the age of thirty-three.

Of course, he had it in his mind to get to the clean chicks, but he also wanted to start the search when he'd be emotionally ready so he could give up all the fucking around and devote himself full-time to the mega investigation. Nowadays he wasn't wasting his sperm for nothing. No! No! No! He was practicing hard so one day he would get his future lady bloated quickly and surely, with first class, premium shots and voilà, have his dream come true. 'Cause Dimitris might have lacked his friend's mega plans for a three room-house and a backyard, but he had another dream to fulfill and that dream had nothing to do with material shit and stuff you lose after your death, that dream would insure his immortality in this vain world so he was working hard to assure it. What's his fucking dream? Simple! Two healthy sons with heavy balls like their baba's. Only two sons and Dimitris's life would be worth the fucking trouble. Dimitris knew it and everybody else knew it. But how do you make Fucking Auntie Puta comprehend a mega plan like this? Definitely not with words. Words were beyond comprehension for Puta or any other fag. Anyway, in general, words were only for coward boys with suits and baba's money. Words arrived when human respect lost its way to the deli store and ended up at the supermarket. Words were not for suburb mega heroes but for fluffy city babes. Actions, actions were the answer to Puta's question and Dimitris was determined to act them out. Mega actions served with ouzo and salted sardines. Actions in all their grandeur. Actions in extra large sizes. That's why the next morning Dimitris hurried to get to the pauper's house 'cause he needed his friend's help in acting out his plan (well, first he had to get a plan but that was a micro-fucking detail). And there was Dimitris in his friend's house gasping out his sporadic breaths and narrating the whole Paradise tale when he realized that the pauper's fly was wide open.

"Zip your store, man. I am here for fucking advice not for an anatomy lesson."

"Fucking red balls," murmured the pauper sealing his treasures, adding, "What the fuck am I supposed to do, man?"

"Huuuu!!!! Huuuu!!!" Dimitris blew a couple of junks of recycled air out of his mouth. Then he patted his chest with his right hand for a minute or so and started the second round of the blah blah. This time the tone of his voice was suppliant, his words extra descriptive.

"Come on man, you have to help me here, my fucking dick is on the butcher's table. You gotta say something. Think! You have a huge brain and a lot of experience in the fucking fuck business. You've done it with the gypsies. Right? How many? Three? Four? Five?"

Silence.

"With how many of them you've done it, dude?"

"Four! But let me reload. It's only eight o'clock in the morning," the pauper hissed and swallowed a mouthful sip of his Turkish coffee.

Long minutes of meditation followed while Dimitris watched his friend scratching his head furiously.

Scratch, scratch! And scratch, scratch. And scratch, scrrrraaaaaaaaaaattccchhhhhhhhh…

Of course there was a purpose for all this scratching but Dimitris failed to catch it so slowly he started sinking into a full depressive mood (head hanging heavy between his hands, eyes in screen saver mode, same thoughts recycling around and around and around).

So ten minutes later when his friend got up over-excited and started shouting, "I got it! I got it! I fucking got it!" Dimitris almost fell off the chair.

"I have the fucking whole act in my mind, man," said the pauper jumping up once more.

"Wow! Dude, I thought I was fucked or something. So, spread it out. I am all ears."

And the pauper with a mysterious conspiratorial tone in his voice started talking and in a few seconds he had landed his mega-plan into Dimitris's lap but it didn't seem that it was comparable to what Dimitris had in mind.

"So, to sum it up, man, what you are saying is that I have to kiss a clean chick in front of Fucking Auntie Puta. Right?" Dimitris asked while his voice revealed several kilos of disappointment.

"That's your fucking big plan, man? That's it? What do you think I am? A magician or something? How do you get a clean chick to land like this in your lap, man? What am I? A gypsy possessing all the demonic tricks of a fucking romantic chapter or something?"

"Relax! Relax! Dude!" the pauper replied trying to calm Dimitris down.

The truth was that the pauper had no idea how Dimitris would execute the proposed plan but he possessed patience, a lot of patience, so he started scratching his head once more and the head responded.

"Look man, you have to grab a chick and kiss her in front of everyone. You don't have to... to... fff..."

"You're a hundred percent on, nothing more," replied Dimitris.

"So, let's start simple. Where do chicks go?"

"Deli, bakery and and and..."

"And the church!" added the pauper without waiting for Dimitris to end his sentence.

"The church!!!" the pauper repeated with a triumphant tone in his voice and a big wide smile.

"So that's where you'll have the scenario acted."

"That's... that's... that's God's house man! Not a premium choice. Is it? That's more like the devil paying a visit to the Virgin Mary or like guaranteeing sin-points or something," Dimitris complained dragging his voice more than usually.

But in a few minutes the pauper easily explained to Dimitris that the church was the coolest place to get something like that accomplished simply because it was the last place that someone would act out something of the kind.

"It's the perfect place to get all the chicks at once dude," the pauper pointed out to Dimitris and Dimitris knew damn well that he was right. All the clean Virgin Maries used to attend church with their families every Sunday so not only Dimitris would be able to prove that he was a man and not a fucking pervert but also prove it using the prop of his desire. He would get to choose whomever he damn well pleased. The plan was to get the preferred chick to the backyard (something difficult that the two friends still had to work out, since the backyard was the smoking area for young men of their manners and not the virgin chicks' playground) and then grab and kiss her on the mouth and voilà: his dick would stand crystal clear once more, forever and ever.

"Hmmm!!! Great stuff man. Feels better than *the great fucking sin*. Better than *the great fucking sin*," Dimitris said with mega satisfaction. "So, next Sunday?"

"Sunday it will be!" agreed the pauper and swallowed the last sip of his coffee.

The Next Sunday (September 1, 1963)

Next Sunday came to be a glorious Sunday, airy, multi-colored, extra-cheerful with mega-blue skies—simply beyond physical or mental boundaries. As a result Agios Nikolas (the only church in the area) got cramped with people. The whole village was there, believers and non-believers, rich and poor, young and old. So the ancient, benevolent, beer-pregnant priest Telonios started his show in great moods, mumbling his sacred words in full excitement (he was the only one who comprehended whatever he was chanting), jerking his frock with one hand and granting his blessings with the other. When he was about to chant his farewell amen, the two protagonists, Pauper (that's his official name from now on) and his old pal Dimitris, made their entrance. A bit more delayed than usually but today was the big day so they were excused by God & Devil. So as soon as they got into their holy chairs, they had to make a u-turn and head for the front yard where the believers were gathering for the weekly social chitchat.

The kiss-plan was already in forward mode and anxiety and enthusiasm were evident on the faces of both protagonists. Dimitris was eyeing the female virgin in the crowd when Pauper whispered into his ear, "Who have we got?"

Dimitris unfolded a piece of napkin where the previous night he had scribbled the names of the three prime chicks of his desire (he couldn't make up his mind which one was the most prime), and after a quick look, he said to his friend, "Toula, Captain Michalis's daughter, but can't see her anywhere," Dimitris's eyes were racing through the fresh flesh.

"Well, maybe she is at her sister's in the capital. So, who do we have next?" Pauper asked once again.

"Chrysa, Master's...."

And before Dimitris ending his sentence, Pauper interrupted him, "Calliga's daughter? You wanna play with fire? She belongs to another division man. Her old man will kill the whole village if his princess gets dirty."

"Well, you said choose. Didn't you? So I did," Dimitris complained.

"You wanna save your dick man? Or throw it into a deeper ditch?"

"She is a prime chick in all dimensions, worth the trouble dude. Look at her," Dimitris insisted half-open mouthed, staring at Chrysa who was walking behind her sisters at that very moment.

The truth was that Pauper had a crush on Chrysa. And his crush was more than an everyday kind of crush. It was a historic crush, going way back to his baba's times. But this was a buried story and digging into it meant a lot of physical and mental work. So he decided to skip it and just murmured between his teeth, "A prime chick alright. A prime fruity chick," while his eyes were following every lingering twist Chrysa's body was performing with exceptional charisma. A minute later when Chrysa got lost behind her oversized sister's rear, Pauper forced an exhalation that went like this, huuuuuu!!!!! Trying to free up his mind from nasty thoughts, he started scratching but this time it was his crotch that needed the scratch and not his head. And scratching his crotch in the presence of the Holy Spirit was something that our hero was not fond of. But what can you do when your lower brain doesn't follow the orders of the upper? You gotta straighten it up regardless of time or place. So he did. And once the scratching business was over, he turned to his friend and asked, "Who else?"

"The... the... the doc's youngest, Petra."

"Petra? She is an infant, man. Only thirteen or something. Same age as my cousin's kid."

"Oh, man, you are difficult. It's my game after all and don't forget that I like them a bit premature so I have time to teach them some discipline and good manners," replied Dimitris smiling wickedly, "and remember a pre-mature babe will go easier to the back, fall for it. So Petra. Let's get my Petra between my...my...hands, dude," Dimitris added with a determined eye looking at Petra who was standing next to her mama and about three meters away from him.

"No, man, it can't be Petra. My cousin will kill me. I am telling you she plays dolls with her little one. She doesn't even know what she got between her legs and you'll grab her like that? And Fucking Auntie Puta won't count Petra for a proper chick so you'll end up scaring the kid for nothing."

"Not for nothing, man, not for nothing," Dimitris said rubbing his hands, sending his good-byes to Petra.

"Well, if you think she won't count in Puta's eyes then we have no choice but to pass her. But then the only one we got is Chrysa and you have to overcome your fears with her so we can proceed. So are you willing to play with Chrysa, yes or no?" Dimitris asked Pauper, trying to make eye contact.

"I am not sure, man. It's a fragile situation like a fine China dish, too expensive and too delicate at once. Let me think for a sec."

And as Pauper was about to get into a thinking mode, at that very moment Chrysa started walking towards the backyard.

"Oh, man, we got no choice. She asks for it. Come on. Let's get to the back before she does," Dimitris hissed in a breath pulling his friend from the arm.

In almost no time, Dimitris and Pauper got themselves to the back. At one end there was Fucking Auntie Puta, rolling his tobacco, humming in low tunes, waiting to witness the promised mega-act. Next to him was Kotsos, Paradise's key holder or simply the Key-holder as they all call him, who came to serve as neutral witness. Next to the Key-holder was Loo, the Key-holder's youngest cousin, the guy with the white pupils and in the middle of the yard were about ten other dudes, thirsty for some romance. Dimitris and Pauper headed for the big pine tree, which was at the other side of the yard, opposite to Puta's and where Chrysa was expected to make her entrance. As soon as the two friends reached the pine's trunk, Chrysa appeared walking carefully on her white shiny pumps while pressing the sides of her embroidered tulle dress with both hands. She looked around as if she were looking for someone and then took a couple of more steps keeping the same rhythm and caution. When she reached the middle of the yard she performed a 360 degree turn and as she was about to make a u-turn heading for the front, Pauper jumped out of nowhere, grabbed her tightly in his arms and pressed his lips on top of hers. Chrysa's white pump slipped off her left foot and landed on the dirt making almost no sound. Just a gentle double toock toock.

The Fruit Basket

We are still in a circle, fuming our *animals* and all when an ancient over-ironed kind of fellow walks in, carrying a mega fruit basket, aiming straight for the bar. It's common knowledge that during these hours no one pays visits to Loo's except us but the fellow doesn't seem to function on local clocks.

"Who is the antique?" I whisper and they all shrug at once.

Antonis kills his Camel and we copy. Maria opens her little bag, pulls out an eau de toilet and spreads some drops into the smoky air. The old man places his basket on the counter and sits on one of the stools at the bar. He takes a deep breath, unbuttons his black suit and eyes the place through his thick glasses.

"Not much change here," he mumbles to himself.

Antonis gets up, walks behind the bar and puts on his working face.

"Anything to drink sir?"

"A beer would be perfect," the old man replies still looking around.

"Are you Loo's son?" he asks while Antonis hands him the cold bottle.

"No. Loo's got no sons, no daughters."

"Do you know what the name of this place was?" the old fellow asks before the bottle reaches his mouth.

"Wasn't after Loo's baba?"

"No," he nods and swallows half of his beer.

"What was it then?" George goes on walking closer to the bar.

"Paradise," the fellow says wiping the foam off his lips.

"Well, did it look like Paradise?" George asks as he sits next to him.

"It looked almost the same as now. Not much change," the fellow replies.

"Now it's called Loo's and it looks like Loo's," Maria adds standing up, heading for the WC.

"Did you use to live here, sir?" Antonis once more.

"No, but I had some clients here so I used to come often."

"When was that?"

"In the early 1960s," the fellow replies and waves the empty bottle to Antonis.

"I guess nothing changes much around here, sir. Only names," Antonis says handing him a second bottle.

"What kind of clients did you have?" I ask.

"I was a lawyer."

"I thought once you are a lawyer; you are always a lawyer."

"Well, yes and no. I haven't been practicing for the last ten years."

"I'll go to law school," I say and sit two stools away from the outsider.

The man turns around and takes a good look at me. And then he asks, "Why do you want to be a lawyer? Why not a teacher or a nurse?"

"'Cause I am not the nurse type and I don't want to be the teacher type," I say feeling glad that I called him antique 'cause his ideas are coming from a thousand years ago.

"How do you know that you are the lawyer type?"

"'Cause her mama tells her so and she possesses a long tongue, perfect for the false blah blah," George replies before I even have a chance to process a thought.

"Well, I like to think I am the type and if not I got the will to get into the type," I finally manage to say.

"That's a smart answer," the fellow says and looks at me as if he has another question in mind but something holds him back, so he says nothing. Then he refocuses from the particular (me) to the general (us) and asks, "So how come you aren't at school?"

"'Cause it's a local holiday. Agios Andreas," Antonis says.

"Oh, that's right. Agios Andreas," the fellow repeats nodding.

"So there is a flea market, right?"

"No. No flea market and bullshit selling. Only food grilling and sausage-stuffing and that's later on, after the religious show is over. So, if you came for a vegetarian meal you wasted your time," George says looking at the fruit basket and we all laugh, including the outsider.

"No, I am not a vegetarian," the old man says, "I'm visiting someone and I don't want to appear empty handed. Not very polite, you know?"

"Of course, of course," Antonis repeats, functioning in agreeable tunes, still working-face on.

George stands up, walks around the fruit basket and takes a thorough look.

"Wow! What have you got here? The four seasons at once. Oranges, cherries, strawberries, bananas, apples..."

"How did you manage to gather Eve's entire garden?"

"Is it the right season for cherries?" Maria asks shaking her wet hands on top of the basket.

"Why? Is it for strawberries?" George goes on circling the basket in slow motion.

"I guess, it isn't but in the city you can find whatever you want, at the time you want it. And after all it looks pretty. Right?"

"Well, pretty doesn't mean tasty. In simple words, an out of season fruit is an out of season fruit. It's like *jumping* for money," Maria adds.

"Multi-colored though. Fills up the eye," Antonis states, sending us the don't-go-out-of-line look.

"Extra multi-colored, like the rainbow," George says gazing at me with his canning eye.

"Yes, yes," the old fellow agrees, sips the last bit of his beer and stands up.

"I am off guys. Thank you for the good company. Gotta go."

He pulls a leather wallet out of his suit packet, leaves a mega-bill on the counter, takes his basket and exits as he entered. Straight ahead.

"So long..."

Antonis rebounds into his normal face. Maria lights an *animal*. And we all smoke. Ten minutes later I get up, pat my empty stomach and say, "I think I should be going home."

"Going for a multi-colored lunch?" Maria requests letting go an over-stretched sarcastic laugh.

"Yeah, an extra colorful one like the rainbow," I say exiting.

"See you around six," George yells, "Eat well. It'll be a long night."

A Swollen Belly

I get it after *jumping*, a temporary swollen belly. I am pretty sure there is a scientific explanation for it but who cares for nerds' views. Anyway, I am lying on George's floor having it, the Camel I mean, waiting for the *jumped*-belly to sag to its normal level and I feel satisfied, knowing that by the end of the last drag I'll be back to normal. So 'till then nothing to do. No moves, no talks. Just enjoying my *animal* waiting for the sperm to lose its hopes and drop dead. And as I am about to suck the last sip, George stands up and starts walking back and forth.

Fuck it, I think but say nothing 'cause I've seen the scene before. He's been playing it for the past couple of months now and it's starting to tether my nerves beyond limits.

Back and forth. Back and forth. Back and forth.

Let's see how long he can last, I think staring at the ceiling.

Back and forth. Back and stop.

This time the walking part of the scene is cut off earlier than usually so I stay put for act two; the whining blah blah, still staring at the ceiling.

"What's up with us?" he asks. Last time he started with, "A drachma for your thoughts?"

"My thoughts aren't so cheap," I said, stood up, got dressed and walked away without watching act three.

"What's up?" he asks again.

"Nothing is up. Ups gone down a few minutes ago," I say smiling but he is not in a comedy mood.

"You know what I mean. What is going on with us?"

He verbalizes the words one by one in extra slow mode as if he is conversing with a retard or something.

"Nothing is up. We just had a pretty good *jump*," I say copying his slow vocalization.

"We made love," he rephrases in extra-fast mode.

"Well, you can call it whatever you like. Fuck, *jump*, love making et cetera, et cetera but it only comes to the same old thing. In & out. In & out," I say dragging the last action words and jerking my right hand to a matching motion.

"Cut it out," he yells.

"Okay. I'll cut it out," I say and stand up looking for my panties and the rest.

"Lately you are acting weird," he goes.

"I am acting as always," I say buckling up my bra.

"It's like you don't care. Do we have something going on here or you started playing in different fields without further notice?" he asks trying extra hard to be cool but his eyes fail him.

"I care," I say slipping into my jeans.

"How much do you care?"

"Well. What can I say? How about thirty kilos? Or you need a bit extra?" I ask.

"Stop fucking around," he shouts and I feel like I've reached my quota for the day so I drop the comedy and "Look, *jumping* is good and I like to do it with you but I don't like the after-drama-section. So, cool it. Enjoy it. Okay? I gotta go now. Later..."

I am heading for the door. George comes for what I think as the-after-*jumping*-kiss but what he is really asking for is a fuck-off-good-bye.

"You have to tell me what we are doing. What do you want from this? Are we having something or not? Are you playing with all your cards on the table or?" he yells and yells on and on for about an infinity, repeating the same shit in different versions, forcing me to evaluate if George-jumping is > than George-whining. And as I am making my calculations, trying to come up with the solution, I look at my belly and it still looks like a pretty fucked up-belly. No normal levels. No, nothing. What is going on? I ask myself without asking George and place my hands on the swollen part. Maybe it's all the fruit I ate after lunch. Maybe the lawyer's basket wasn't so good after all. Maybe he had in mind to poison someone and it wasn't left for mama as I assumed. Maybe he mixed up the houses and he just left it outside our door thinking that it was the door of an old client of his who hadn't paid for his service. Maybe...

"You have to answer me. Now. At this very moment. No more games."

I hear George's voice going through my swollen belly and I know that if I don't lock myself in the toilet in the next ten minutes we'll be having a pretty shitty split.

"Look, I gotta go. Let's resume later," I say and exit heading home in a careful-quick mode, holding my belly with both hands, exhaling/inhaling in equal intervals like a real yogi.

The Feast

Same day, around ten p.m. I just managed to get my belly back to normal levels, heading for the village square now where the mega sausage feast has been going on for the last couple of hours. There is a bursting smelly cloud of roasted meat covering the whole central area of the square, some horrible folk music going on and full attendance, even people from other villages have shown up to celebrate Agios Andreas's day. I locate mama seating next to Wicked Yiayia and Kyra Margarita, that's our mega nurse and Stare-Cat No One. Their table is pretty close to the dancing floor and pretty far from the folklore band where baba and his fellows are parked drinking, eating, and laughing all at once. It's the third time I see baba in the last months. He looks older, fatter, and happier. Wicked Yiayia sees me, starts swinging her hands trying to get my attention so in no time I make a u-turn heading for the opposite direction. Everybody swings in elevated alcoholic moods. Too bad that almost-full-time-drunk-pappoo has gone to heaven and isn't around to enjoy the insobriety, I think as I try to get lost behind the huge BBQ grill. There is meat, meat and more meat on top of the grill. Certainly not a vegetarians' day!

"Sunday. Sunday." I hear from somewhere someone calling but I proceed without checking for the originator.

"Sunday, Sunday," once again in a more aggressive tune now. Who the hell is that? I wonder trying to recognize the voice or the tone but the over-crowded roasted atmosphere doesn't let me so I turn around eyeing through fuming meat.

"My Sunday," the voice comes from where I didn't expect it in sweet lingering tunes along with a smooth patting on my left shoulder. So now I am face to face with this elegant, out-of-place-woman who looks too familiar to me but I fail to recall her name. I open my eyes a bit more, hoping to turn on memory channels but nothing comes out of it, just more roasted smoke, so I am forced to go blink-blink and blink once again. The woman must think that I am a bloody blind idiot, but the woman seems to have a normal functioning flow of reasoning so she says "It's Mrs. Dimou, Sunday. Remember? Your mama's friend from New York. I just arrived a few hours ago with Bo. I am looking for your mama. You've grown up so much. It was difficult to recognize you. Such a pretty girl," she goes on smiling revealing extra-white, over-shiny teeth in perfect alignment.

"She is over there," I say stretching my pointer in front of her face.

"Great, great!" she nods and walks away.

When I finally manage to snap out of it (the stupid mode I mean), the elegant woman has already reached mama's table and she is in the second round of kisses and hugs and more of the kind. I start walking once again and a few minutes later I locate my group of friends, seating in a table next to the garbage cans, in a safe territory, far enough from parental visibility. There is Maria, Antonis and where I expect to see George I locate a dark brown head of long straight hair that I am not sure to whom it belongs since it's facing the other way.

"Ah!! Here she is," Maria says pointing with her cunning look at me and Antonis with the unidentified head turn around at once.

"Hey, you made it," Antonis says and the other head stands up and gives me a squeeze along with an over-warm unexpected kiss.

"Hey Bo," I manage to verbalize, amazed, thinking that the Bo I remembered was fifty kilos uglier comparing to the one I am squeezed by at this very moment. I guess our thoughts crossover and without wasting any time he asks, "What did you take girl?" And immediately after he sends me a meaningful look, the kind I am supposed to pretend not to comprehend but since I am a *weird chick functioning like possessing balls and all the manly sweat* as Antonis believes, I act accordingly. So I give him an extra-welcome-kiss, resting almost accidentally on his tender lips, openly revealing that I got the message and have already filed it properly in my short future plans file.

"You are three sizes larger and ten times prettier," he adds and it's a totally suitable remark but as I am about to keep up the stirring flirtatious code, George cuts us off.

"Here are the drinks," he states with exceptional eagerness and forced enthusiasm as if he is imitating Columbus's reaction in front of America. He hands us the Amstels with an over-joyous smile and suggests, "To Bo," rising up his bottle.

"To Bo," Maria and Antonis follow suit.

"To Bo," I say putting on an I-don't-give-a-fuck look determined to swallow as much as I can in the hope of making a good impression and douse off mental and emotional thirst.

The next couple of hours are wasted on English vocab, beer drinking and eye flirting. Needless to say that the latest and best act is only shared between Bo and me, happily observed by Maria and Antonis and seriously opposed by George who makes an extra effort to declare our *jumping* habits placing his hands all around my shoulders, legs, waist and wherever he can get a grasp of. A fucking embarrassing, most humiliating gaucherie if you ask my sincere opinion.

"Give us another word for tsootsoo," Antonis requests from Bo who is the official English expert now. The NJY (New *Jumping* Yorker) as we all call him.

"Tsootsoo?" Bo repeats while processing in the back of his head the possible meaning of the word.

"Tsoo-tsoo. It's like all the dual-beat words; ma-ma, ba-ba. Tsoo square simply makes tsootsoo," Maria offers to explain with a serious tone in her voice as if she is solving a mathematical problem, while Antonis supplements her attempt grabbing his crotch, and looking straight into Bo's eyes who by now seems to have comprehended it all.

"So you mean dick?" Bo says, jerking his head up and down.

"Dick? I've said nothing about your baba man. I only ask for another version for our fucking private mega-male organ."

"Well, they call it dick. Dick with a small d is another word for tsoot-soo. And Dick with a capital D is a name and surprisingly enough it happens to be also my father's nickname. It's the same word for both."

"Fucking hell," Antonis giggles embarrassed, "that's pretty nasty, man. They call your baba tsootsoo? Why? Does he possess a mega huge one or something?"

"No. No. They don't just call my father that. It's a nickname for Richard. So they usually call Richards: Dick. You see it has nothing to do with the other meaning of the word."

"Once again this shows that Americans have no imagination. They don't even bother to create another word for our mega tool," George states, releasing a cunning gaze while grabbing my thighs with his beer-free hand.

"Well it's like calling you Sunday," Bo continues turning at my side.

"I must confess Sunday is a pretty bad name but still it's better than vagina or something. Don't you think?" I question with a lingering erotic gaze.

"Sunday instead of Vaaa-giii-naaa..." Bo says overstretching the last three syllables trying to look skeptical instead of drunk.

"Is there another word for it?" Maria interrupts him.

"For what?"

"For tsootsoo, man. For tsootsoo," she adds.

"Yes, there is. It's cock. But it is a harsh word."

"Kock? With a K?" she asks once again.

"No. Cock with a C. C-o-c-k," Bo spells out.

"That sounds bigger than a dick to me," Antonis says and we all burst laughing.

"It's only harder," Bo adds and swallows the rest of his beer, still gazing at my side.

"So cock. That's a good one," Maria says rethinking the word in the back of her head, bigger and harder than ever.

"And how would you say *take me a pipe* in official English?" George asks.

"That's a blowjob, man," Maria interrupts before even Bo has a chance to say anything.

"That's right."

"Well, well! Someone is an expert in this one," I say and Maria gives me a shut-up look.

"How about you teach your friend some of your expertise, Maria?" George jumps from nowhere, squeezing my hand now. I try to overpass his nailing remark but my mind has already recorded it in the revenge file.

Antonis senses my anger and quickly proposes, "How about if we drop the English lesson for now and go for a vegetarian meal, guys?"

"That's great," we all agree and in no time we cover our red plastic plates with huge sausages.

"Let's eat our cocks, guys," Maria giggles biting a big piece of her overcooked sausage.

Disgusting! I say without using any vocab, just a facial grimace while tearing off a delicious juicy piece of mine.

A Machiavellian Approach

I arrive home around one in the morning in hip moods. Simply happily lightheaded and successfully well fed. I guess all the sausages, Amstels, Camels and erotic eyebeams seem to work miracles, I think, as I tiptoe heading for my room, trying to avoid any unpleasant motherly scenes. But before reaching my salvation, a foreign male voice coming from the living room stops me. Who is that? At this hour? I wonder pausing at once and stretching out my antennas.

"It's your call now, Chrysa. You have the choice to change your life once and for all. Now you are a smart woman. You have experienced what love can and cannot bring," the voice states in a heavy, lethargic tone.

Who is that man that calls mama by her name? I question myself once more in full silence. For a moment I hear nothing. Only my own breath. Mama follows one of her famous meditation techniques, says nothing till she hears what she wants to, I think but as soon as I finish my thought I hear her reply. In a staccato determined tone, which is pretty foreign to me, "You know my answer, so please leave."

And then once again deep silence. What the hell is going on? I think while my curiosity is overhead. So I decide to unpause and take a couple of steps towards the living room with the hope to get a quick view of the man in question.

And voilà. Here to my great surprise once again is the fruit basket lawyer! Wow!

I've seen enough of you in one day, I think, wondering how come I fail to recognize his voice. He is wearing the same black suit but looks about three kilos younger plus five kilos taller than at the Loo's place. It's as if he has ironed some of his wrinkles off and as an after-effect he got a couple of extra centimeters added to his height. Great ironing, I think stepping back to my pausing spot.

"Well, think about it. And remember I don't have a lot of time," he says.

Then I hear no words. Just steps. Then the door opens and closes. The antique evaporates; I resume and take a few steps towards my room. I turn the knob of my door and in secs I am flat on my bed staring at the moving ceiling.

To think or not to think? I question. There isn't an easy response to that. It's nothing like *to-jump-or-not-to-jump?* Where you just take a look at your panties and if moist you go on with it, if not you withdraw. *Jumping* questions have straightforward genuine answers. Thinking requires much more than that. First of all it requires a clean crystal head, something I lack at this very moment. And then to think about mama, the antique mystery man, Wicked Yiayia, baba, and all the domestic melodrama is something totally unpleasant, so I decide to drop the serious thinking for the next chapter and go on with what lays next to *jumping*. And what lies next to *jumping?* Come on! That's an easy one. *Hand-wash!* Remember? Or as Bo has said, using the official English terminology: masturbation.

Masturbation, I verbalize slowly. What a word. Full in length and totally non-descriptive, I think and, a few minutes later, I find myself in the middle of the room flipping through the English dictionary. I read,

> *"Masturbation (mas-tur-ba'shon) n. manipulation of the genitals for sexual gratification."*

A first-class, premium explanation, if you ask me. Imprecisely vague and gently indistinct. Well, well, I really like Americans. They definitely leave space for our imagination to flourish. Just come to a sexual gratification, we don't give a damn how you do it. Just do it. Hands, fingers and other fleshly and not-so-fleshly parts line up for full use. A pretty Machiavellian approach, I think. Viva America! The Greatest Masturbator of all. Filled with every color, religion, nationality et cetera, et cetera, I mumble, lying on my bed. That heroic thought is my last for the night. And there goes my memory along with my masturbation plans, turning off unexpectedly like mega-sudden power-cuts.

And abracadabra! Magic!!! Next morning is here. I don't remember seeing a more annoyingly anxious sun than the one outside my window. It seems definitely overcharged and extra determined to get through my room curtains, my sheets and my eyelids. What a blessing, mama would have said if she were to witness it. But thank GG; she is occupied, boiling coffee for her New Yorker friend, Mrs. Dimou, who has arrived for an annual report bringing me a pretty cool New York City T-shirt and a Calvin & Hobbes Book. So I put on my new T-shirt, place Calvin under my shoulder and lock myself in the bathroom leaving mama and her friend chatting happily around the kitchen table. A perfect morning I think to myself as I park my rear cheeks on top of the toilet opening Calvin &

Hobbes on my thighs. So I start reading getting deeper and deeper into Calvin's mental coo, starting to feel relaxed, extra-content, the happy-cow-brand, if you know what I mean. But as soon as I get about two kilos of relaxation I hear some pretty strong words coming out of the kitchen, so I leave Calvin aside for a sec, trying to grasp a complete sentence.

"...Maidenhead...worries...don't think about it...he wanted to marry a virgin...you gave him what he wanted...well, you gotta..."

That's all I can make out, so I reach and open the door hoping for a better reception, but I end up with a similar verbal sample in a slightly different order. And as I am thinking that if I were unrestrained of physical laws, I would have left my butt on top of the toilet and send my eyes and ears to the next room, a clear-crystal sentence flies into my head.

"Sixteen years ago you managed pretty well and now you are worried over a simple blood test? Oh come on, Chrysa, focus on the doughnut and stop staring at the hole."

And little by little all the previous unorganized words start playing a sad tune in my head and I feel my cow-contentedness flashing down the toilet like a tiny little piece of shit. Fucking hell. I can't enjoy a simple morning without having the past blowing all over my face, I think, as Calvin & Hobbes return to their two-dimensional black and white state.

Dimitris's Reaction

So immediately after the mega kiss plus Mrs. Calliga's scene, there was Dimitris's reacting. And although at first Dimitris's reacting was just a semi-aggressive blended, cocktail verbal blah-blah, in the end, it became a painful bloody incident. And here is what I mean.

"Fuck man? What happened? You, you...grabbed her? And...and... where did the mama come from?" Dimitris uttered as Pauper was making his way up, rubbing the dust off his pants with both hands.

"You are in deep shit," Fucking Auntie Puta said who was now standing next to Dimitris along with the Key-holder, Loo and the rest of the boys staring at the rising hero.

"Was that improvising or?" Puta went on gazing from Dimitris to Pauper and reverse but got no replies.

"What did you do that for?" Dimitris went on, "I thought I was the...the..."

"The fucking fool?" Fucking Auntie Puta added releasing a mega sarcastic laugh and all copied minus Pauper and Dimitris.

"What happened, man?" Dimitris asked once more. This time too loud.

"Are you blind, man? He kissed the chick. He grabbed her and gave her a mega wet kiss on the lips. Mats moots! Or it was more like mooootsssss?" the Key-holder mocked while demonstrating the moves; over-swinging his head to one side and his arms to the other and releasing kisses into the breezy air. At that very moment Dimitris took one more step, standing now face to face with his friend, too close to be dismissed and asked, "What's your story, man? Explain your fucking act or I will…"

And without any verbal continuation a puuufff went off as Dimitris's fist stroke Pauper's left cheek with extra enthusiasm and mega determination. For one more time Pauper found himself on the holy dirt but this time things weren't looking so bright. Actually they were looking pretty bloody; his nose was bleeding, his head was spinning around and around. For a minute our hero closed his eyes and tried to refocus but in vain. The spinning got faster. So he gave up and passed out with style: hands holding forehead, releasing an extra long breath while bending slowly towards one side.

"You killed him, man. You killed him," the Key-holder yelled standing on top of Pauper along with the rest of the boys.

Dimitris's gaze changed from hard to soft to anxious in fast-forward speed. How did I do that? He questioned himself bending over his friend's bloody face.

"We gotta get him to Stella's," the Key-holder yelled bending all the way and grabbing Pauper's arms.

"Okay guys. Let's move it," they all agreed in a single voice.

Cross-Stitching

A few minutes later…

"I will give you my best handwork pretty boy but you gotta hold it still. Be a man. No fidgeting. No nothing. Okay?"

"Okay," Pauper nodded as mega-nurse Stella was rubbing with alcohol her shiny long needle.

"Cross-stitching for pretty brave boys like yourself, it's my specialty. You know? You know how many cheeks I've put together over the years? Well. Well. Many. Too many. Front and back ones. If you know what I mean," she said smiling and aiming for Pauper's skin.

"Ay! Ayyyy!!! Virgin Mary," Pauper cried out as the needle went through his flaming cheek.

"No talking. No nothing. Didn't we say? Show your manhood, boy," mega-nurse Stella said once more as she was executing her craftwork with extra smooth moves.

"Don't faint on me now! Hold it. Just one more pretty bow and we are done," she went with an almost signing tune in her voice while Pauper was reaching gigantic dimensions of pain.

"Take a look. Four little bows. One next to the other. Isn't that pretty or what?" Mega-nurse Stella asked Pauper with enthusiasm holding a mirror in front of his face.

"Looks better than it feels. That's for sure," he mumbled gazing at his reflection.

"Of course it does. And now I'll let Margarita here do the cleaning up," Mega-nurse Stella said as micro nurse Margarita was approaching with a handful of cotton.

"In no time you will be in your way. I just got to clean up the blood," Margarita said wiping up Pauper's skin with extra caution.

"I hope you gave as much as you got," Margarita added for Pauper to reply but got nothing out of his mouth.

"Well, a fight is a fight and you have to fight it back. Right?" Margarita went on once again after pausing her moves for a sec.

But Pauper held on to his mute-daytime dreaming act; stone face on, focusing on faraway scenes.

"But isn't it kind of weird? One day you can be like brothers with someone and the next day you end up in a fist fight. Dimitris is your best buddy, right?" Margarita asked looking at Pauper.

"News travels in light-speed. Eh?"

"It's a small village we got. People care for each other. You know how it goes," she replied.

"So what else do you care to know about?" Pauper asked Margarita as he was staring at her broad v-neck.

"Well, nothing else. But isn't it weird that you go for a holy blessing and you end up with four stitches on your beautiful face?" she asked pretending to ignore Pauper's wandering gaze, bending on top on his face, exhibiting more melon flesh.

"I say more lucky than weird, being here, having you taking care of me," Pauper mumbled in a vigorous hypnotic tone resting his head on Margarita's verandas, wearing a pseudo-dizzy look and forcing a full-size exhale.

"Cough, cough. Time is up," mega nurse Stella went interrupting the smooching scene.

"Your friends are at the hall so next time choose another day. Sunday is for resting not for messing around," she yelled sending a get-away look at Margarita.

Pauper stood up and headed for the door slowly trying to think of a good explanation to face up his pal Dimitris and the rest of the dudes. But lucky, lucky he was, Dimitris was already gone when our hero appeared with his pretty stitches in front of the rest of the boys. Mega questioning took place but nothing important was really revealed. After all Pauper wasn't going to publish his inner wounds to Fucking Auntie Puta or to any other fuck hungry for local drama. And it wasn't because he didn't believe in sharing. On the contrary he was a big sharing believer. Share your pain with your friends and you will feel half of it, share your happiness and you'll be double happy, that was our hero's mantra but surprise, surprise for the first time in his life he was left alone without a tight buddy, without a real friend and he wasn't feeling his usual self.

From Left to Right (Wednesday, September 4, 1963)

D o you use your left or right for a *hand-wash*? (Write your answer below. No one is looking).

Well, now let me rephrase the question: Do you think it would make a mega difference (in other words be better), if your left hand were executing the job while your right was watching? Or vice-versa? (You don't have to answer this one. Pauper will).

So, after many years of *hand-wash* and a lot of switching around (left to right, right to left et cetera), Pauper realized one thing: that he could and had trained both of his hands to execute the job equally well (simply reach the highest levels of pleasure), but he couldn't, although he tried effortlessly, accomplish to perform the job at the same speed. Left was always working in slow motion. Right was never able to slow down. So as far as Pauper was concerned left was used when there was plenty of time and right when there wasn't. So three days after the famous kiss, Wednesday morning, when Pauper woke up and found no one around,(his mama was across the street at the neighbor's house, his baba totally drunk at the usual dry ditch), he thought that it was a perfect day for a *hand-wash* and since there was plenty of time he unzipped his store, took out his tsootsoo with the left hand and started the job in a slow steady motion. But as he was about to enter the rinsing cycle he heard a weird noise.

"Click, click."

He looked around, saw nothing and went on. But a few seconds later the weird noise got weirder.

"Tink, click, clack."

He quickly switched from left to right, and finished up in no time. Then without wiping off the extra bubbles, he closed up his store and walked towards the window where the noise was coming from. There he saw Kyra Sophia, bent over on top of the semi-dirt semi-asphalt road, looking for another stone to shoot into his window. When Kyra Sophia bounced back into her vertical position and saw Pauper at the window, she dropped the stone and signaled him to come down. Pauper's house was on the first floor, and below was an abandoned old garage. Kyra Sophia waved with her left hand while holding tightly something with the right. Pauper couldn't possibly imagine what she was about to give him (at the moment his imagination was switched off), so in no hurry he passed by the sink to rinse off both hands and slowly started going down the stairs humming an ethnic popular tune, "Greece will never die. Greece will live forever. Greece…"

When he opened the door he found Kyra Sophia in fuming moods. Too serious, too annoyed and in a mega rush. "I am putting my life in danger here and you are mumbling like a fool. Anyway what took you so long?"

"Well, I …I…was…"

"Look I am not here for apologies. My Miss gave me this. You are supposed to read it and then eat it up. Destroy it. Vanish it. Comprende?"

Pauper nodded without really comprehending what he was agreeing to.

"I'll be back for the reply, tomorrow, same time," she said and went off.

Pauper took a good look at the mystery object, which was really just an over-moist pinkish flowery envelope and then started climbing up the stairs one by one in full silence. No hums. No nothing. Only an extra skeptical look, with eyebrows pointing tenaciously at the third eye but seeing nothing. When he reached the last step, he looked back, making sure he was totally solo, got in, locked the door behind him, opened the envelope and read,

My dearest,

From that day on, I cannot sleep. You are in my thoughts.
It was so brave from you to act upon your feelings and express your
love in such an unforeseen but absolutely convivial way.
I want you to know that I do share similar feelings and as long as
you stand by my side I will do everything to keep our love alive.
I will be waiting for your reply.

Forever yours,
Chrysa.

Full of Shit

In the last days Master Calliga had made serious attempts to empty his personal SC (Shit Closet) but failed big time. So on Wednesday after reaching desperately vulnerable moods, left with zero kilos of pride and an overloaded belly, he had no choice but beg for Divine help. Thus as soon as he entered the WC he started searching with his eyes for the brown leather-cover holy book usually placed next to the toilet. A few seconds later, unable to locate it, Master freaked out. So reasonably enough he started yelling, "Woman, where did you put it? Answer me, woman. Why isn't it here?"

When Mrs. Calliga heard her husband's barks, she knew exactly what to look for and where. Thus she ran from the living room where she was, to the bedroom, reached under her pillow, grabbed the object in search and headed for the bathroom in full speed.

"Stop shouting like a madman. Here it is," she said as she handed it to her husband, who at that very moment was taking his royal seat, pants and drawers pulled down all the way.

"Why the hell do you take it from here? I've told you a thousand times, it helps me concentrate," he whined expecting the same old good reply in the same old good flat tone.

And as programmed for the thousandth time Mrs. Calliga went on, "This is not the place for this kind of book. God forgive us. God ..." she started mumbling while jerking her mega hairdo slowly from left to right and walking away.

In the mean time Master Calliga was flipping through the pages of Genesis, trying to locate the right passage while exhaling big chunks of air with great effort, hoping for the catharsis process to start any minute. And soon enough the Divine's great powers released him. So a catharsis began in abrupt explosions of semi-solid lumps, creating weird sounds.

"Amen! Amen!" Master murmured to himself with great relief a couple of times, letting the holy book slip off his fingers. When the scatological bombing reached its peak, Master's face was in full bliss, all red and sweaty. And it was at that very moment when the great idea hit Master's brain, decorating his face with an extra-stretched smile.

"I have the solution. What a match! What a redemption!" he shouted in full enthusiasm to himself.

Ten minutes later when he was about to start eating his usual breakfast (a salad bowl filled with milk and pieces of bread), he put on his genius look and with low voice, cunning gaze and mega confidence he started revealing his great idea to his wife.

"How old is he?" Mrs. Calliga asked after hearing her husband's plan.

"What difference does it make?" Master replied, ready to go on with his narration.

"Well, I don't want him to be older than you are."

"He is not older. He is about ten years younger than me. He is your age," Master replied at once looking straight into Missus's eyes.

And immediately after he continued, "What is it? He is prefect for Chrysa. He is a lawyer. We need a lawyer in the family. He'll be perfect for her. Drop that sour look."

"Maybe you are right," Mrs. Calliga said hesitantly.

"No maybes, I am always right. Who will take her after what she's done? Who? Or you want to give her to one of them? My daughter in the hands of a poor, muddy, dirty creature...like like those..."

"No, of course not," Mrs. Calliga agreed with him.

"So let's plan a dinner. When do you want to have it? This Saturday? The faster the better for our name. I want to be able to go to the tavern without mud dripping off my face. I'll invite him Saturday. Okay? Saturday?" he asked once more at the very moment Kyra Sophia was serving his coffee.

"Isn't it too soon?" Mrs. Calliga questioned in confusion.

"Soon? No. It's perfect. Saturday! Have everything ready and I'll get him here. And make sure she looks good. Buy her a new dress or something," he said resolutely and took a mega sip of his coffee.

About an hour later Kyra Sophia was exiting Chrysa's room with an empty tray in her hands and a love letter hidden between her sweaty big balloons. But as she was cutting through the living room, Mrs. Calliga stopped her.

"So how is our little princess? Did she dry off her fake mega tears or is she going on with her show?" Mrs. Calliga asked Kyra Sophia ironically eyeing the tray.

"Well... I don't think she is faking. I think that...that..." Kyra Sophia went on hesitantly.

"You think what? I know very well how you think Sophia. I know all your clever ideas. Once I was almost ruined because of your clever ideas. Remember?" Mrs. Calliga stretched her vocal cords to their limits, her raised eyebrows reaching for her hairline.

"Look at me Sophia," Mrs. Calliga ordered once again taking a couple of steps backwards and extending her forefinger in front of Kyra Sophia's face, "Stay out of this. Don't try to fill Chrysa's head with the same bs you tried to fill mine. Don't mess up with her fate, 'cause if you do, I give you my word, no one will stop me from kicking you out of this house. No one. You hear me? Not even my mama's mega spirit. Got it?"

"What's all this? I...I... don't understand...I," Kyra Sophia complained while trying to follow with her eyes Missus's pointer, which was shaking in high speed.

"Sophia, you know damn well what I mean. Just because you were my mama's favorite don't think that you can do whatever you please. I am telling you once more, don't mess with Chrysa's life," Mrs. Calliga ordered. Then she walked away.

Kyra Sophia stood in the middle of the living room for several seconds trying to rearrange the thoughts in her head and the love letter in her deep cleft, which was by now getting extra-moist. Then she made a u-turn and headed for the mega brick kitchen located on the lower lever of the Calliga Mansion. She entered the room still lost in her thoughts but in no time she had to snap out of them and face Georgia's and Maro's vexations. Georgia was the mega matriarch of the Calliga family. Maro was her bastard who had inherited Georgia's cursing habits, succulent breasts, and forced giggles, but lacked all the gastronomic expertise her mama was famous for.

"Damn it. Bloody stupid dinners for nothing," Georgia was moaning as she was reading through a long grocery list to Maro who was checking the cabinets with clumsy moves and great annoyance.

"What's going on?" Kyra Sophia asked.

"We are having a mega dinner on Saturday," Maro replied slamming one of the cabinet doors.

"THEY are having a dinner on Saturday. WE are just cooking it. Working our asses off for nothing," Georgia said.

"Who is coming?" Kyra Sophia inquired, reaching between her breasts.

"Don't know," Georgia mumbled.

"A big shot. We are cooking lamb, chicken, rabbit and making four kinds of sweets," Maro added forcing a long breath.

"That's definitely a mega-huge-shot," Kyra Sophia agreed skeptically while at the same time she was replaying fragments of the conversation she had just heard while serving coffee to the Master. But before she could reach any significant conclusions Maro interrupted her.

"What you got there?" she asked, looking at the crumpled piece of paper that came out of Kyra Sophia's boobs.

"Nothing."

"Don't nothing me, smart-ass." Georgia jumped and in no time grabbed the paper out of Kyra Sophia's hands.

"It isn't for you, Georgia. Don't put your dirty nose in others' business," Kyra Sophia objected, but it was too late. Georgia was almost through reading when Kyra Sophia managed to get it back.

"You will get in an extra-mega mess if Missus finds out what you are about to do. And I won't be around to protect you. And if it reaches Master's ears...forget it! You better have your shroud ready to meet the rest of the sinners in Hades."

"No one will find out," Kyra Sophia said looking straight at Georgia's sparking gaze as if she were sending her a keep-your-mouth-shut look.

"I am dead. Don't look at me. And my Maro here has a zipped-up mouth. But don't forget walls have ears," Georgia assured Kyra Sophia and went back to her grocery list.

Kyra Sophia picked up the kitchen cloth, which was hanging from Georgia's apron, unbuttoned the first few buttons of her robe and slowly started wiping off her soggy hanging balloons. When she finished, she replaced the love letter between her deep cleft, handed the cloth to Georgia, and exited the kitchen with determined steps.

Where was she heading? Well, we already know that one.

The Morning of the Mega Dinner (Saturday, September 7, 1963)

It is 5:34, Saturday morning. The first rays of light enter the mega sky one after the other in full speed, strong and unsuspected. A dead rabbit and a defrosted chicken are hanging upside-down naked and empty-stomached from the kitchen's ceiling. Their dripping blood makes steady rhythmic sounds (toock, toock, toock), splashing half on the floor and half on a skinless lamb leg, which rests directly beneath them on the wooden kitchen counter.

Master Calliga opens his eyes, his head still on the pillow. Without much movement he forces a dry cough, eyeing his wife who is lying on the other end of the bed in an S shape, mega rear sticking out in all directions.

"Cough! Cough! Cough!" Three more identical fake coughs and then he grasps his balls as if he is checking their weight. Two, three, maybe more kilos of racing blood between his hands. He is satisfied. What a mega shooter he is. If it were only a bit later, he would have been able to unload his mega bullets between Maro's tender thighs. Well. Well. *Damn it. What can I do?* He questions in full silence. Big mega rear will do. For fifteen-sixteen years now he has been using Missus's *back door*. You see, after four kids, her *front door* doesn't seal properly. Anyway, not as it used to. And an improperly sealed *front door* doesn't do much. Just hangs there, collecting dust. And since there isn't a holy purpose anymore in loading his bullets, (one *child* and three girls are enough), but just pure pleasure, he doesn't mind performing from the back. On the contrary, he's being released of viewing hanging breasts, belly folds and hollow gazes. He rides while his mind fantasizes fresh rosy lips murmuring no, no, no. Like a pleasant ride in a Cadillac while listening to the radio on an over-used asphalt road, with no bad surprises.

"Cough! Cough! Cough!" he repeats, once more holding his tsoot-soo with one hand while with the other trying to set his target into a suitable angle.

"Ooohhh! Where do you find the courage?" Missus mumbles, still half asleep.

"Come on, woman, hold up your nightie now," Master Calliga orders her between unsettled breaths.

"Here you go my old mare." He pushes happily with all his strength grabbing his target from the waist with both hands.

It was almost like yesterday when the mayor asked him, "You do it in the doggy style Master, right?"

"Doggy style?" he wondered. He knew no doggy style, no nothing. He had already three daughters but was still too young and naïve for things like that.

"I only know about farming 'cause my baba has trained me well, but about that sort of thing I am in deep dark," he confessed to the mayor without making eye contact.

"No wonder you got only girls," the mayor replied.

And then with a loud laugh he added, "Doggy style for Greeks and Greek style for Americans. SSS, Simply Same Shit!"

Master Calliga's imagination was shook once and forever. As soon as he got home he grabbed his Missus from the back and there he was doing it in the doggy style. Nine months later he was holding his *child* in his arms.

Bloody hell, he thought, *if I only knew this earlier I'd have got three children and a daughter by now.* Not the other way around. But anyway he was happy and knew that he owed many thanks to the mayor so he bought a big bottle of Metaxa, with seven golden stars one next to the other, and rushed to pay him a visit, showing off his gratitude. It was then that the mayor told him about the sneaky style.

"Sneaking like a thief from the *back door*," he said laughing and patting him on the shoulder. And although it took him a good year to convince Missus to let him go through her *back door* when he finally did it there was no way to get him back to normal.

"What a road!" he murmured to his friend with a mega smile hanging off his wet lips.

"What a narrow twisty little alley!" the mayor laughed, as they were finishing up another Metaxa bottle. This was a five-star. Seven-star was only for a once-in-a-lifetime-event and sneaky style wasn't going to be one of those. Sneaky style was going to be the weekly style. The only style for the Master.

"Foo! Foo!" the Master gasps laying flat on his back.

Missus slips off the bed in a rush, shooting a taut couple of farts in high volume.

"Devil's work," she mumbles. The truth is that by now she has gotten used to it. No hurting no nothing. But the farts, she can't tolerate. They go on and on and on, without stopping, in dancing, stinking duos for at least four to five hours after the dirty act. It's as if they want to say something. They want to inform the whole world that he is tearing her apart for no apparent reason.

"Tell Georgia I want a proper breakfast with sausages, eggs, toast and fruit. I worked for it. No?" the Master says with a cunning smile.

Missus releases a couple more farts and exits the room.

Georgia is already in the kitchen when Missus arrives. She is anxious to start up cooking 'cause today is the day of the big shot's dinner. Kyra Sophia has managed to uncover some of the mystery details about the mega dinner.

"A rich fellow from the capital is coming to take a look at the youngest," she says to Georgia and Maro, "the Master is anxious to get rid of her before she loses her golden shiny looks and become like the oldest one. Poor Zoë…"

"Before she gets her mama's wide rear, right?" Maro laughs, covering her mouth with both hands.

"Watch your mouth young lady," Georgia says and then turns to Kyra Sophia, "but I thought she loves the other fellow. The one who wrote the letter for."

"That's history. Only if she wants to get hanged," Kyra Sophia replies in a mega dark crap mood. Georgia understands that's the end of the story, so she goes back to her cooking, big tears running down her face.

"All those years and I can't get used to onion-cutting. I'm an onion victim," she says nodding lethargically.

"Oh, Georgia! It only means that nature is larger than us. Larger!" Kyra Sophia reassures her.

"Your Master fancies a big breakfast today," Missus orders Georgia, "Leave the rabbit for now and cook a couple of sausages. I'll boil eggs."

"Yes, my Missus," Georgia replies assigning her daughter to get the sausages.

A half hour later the Master is on his last bite. Georgia is back to her rabbit, stuffing its belly with scallions and poking a leaf of basil in each eye. Kyra Sophia is in the youngest's room. And Missus is in the living room with the two oldest drinking her usual morning coffee.

"Baba never thinks of me?" Zoë states, working her whining high-pitched voice in medium tone.

"Baba thinks about all of us," Mrs. disagrees.

"So where is my husband then?" Zoë replies in protesting mood, eyebrows fully erect, lower lip hanging heavily.

And without waiting for her mama she continues, "I am the oldest. I should get married first."

"You will dear. You're the bravest. The neatest. And your baba knows it. You know how difficult it is for me to let you go. You know how I feel about it." These last few sentences are dipped in honey, sugar and all the dulcet ingredients. Smooth! Sweet!

"And me? How about me? If Zoë is first then I am second!" Sunday jumps from nowhere into the conversation.

"Oh! Please don't start, Sunday. I am talking with your sister now," Missus complains and gulps the rest of her coffee.

"It's always the same story. When Zoë talks no one can say a word. It's Zoë or no one. Right?"

"You know what I think, Sunday?" Zoë interrupts her sister with furious intentions. But Missus is in no mood for one of their girlish verbal battles so she settles the order in no time, banging the floor with both heels and releasing her aromatic body ventilations in loud rapid duos which go like this: prit-prit and prit-prit.

"That's it girls. That's the end of it. And, Sunday, stop eating the cookies. Now both of you go and help Georgia."

"Ohh mama! Your stomach problem again. I've told you, you should visit the doctor. I am sure there is something he can do about that," Zoë remarks covering her nose with her handkerchief.

"There is nothing wrong with my stomach. Nothing wrong," Missus says rubbing her right double-D tit with both hands.

Kiss My Ass

In my time girls *were getting married virgins.*
In my time boys lived for the first night of their wedding.
In my time people fell in love.
In my time...
That was mama's time. The best of the best, the fairytale type of time. But my time?

My time is a pile of mega shit. The whorehouse. The Chinatown of every big city. *Can't you see? It's not my fucking fault. It's yours. You created me in that time. I had nothing to do with it*, I repeat and repeat and repeat, but mama doesn't capture the meaning of my words. Mama doesn't feel responsible for the timing of my birth. Mama runs a different algorithm in her head along with all other mamas in the world. And baba? Well baba is out of the frame. Baba is a man with balls, and as far as he is concerned he has done his part; shot up his bullets and finito, that was it for him. So I'm living in my time; only a suicide can set me free from that and I am not the suicide type, and every minute that passes gets me farther and farther from mama's time and here is mama to remind me of that.

In my time girls didn't dress like that.
In my time girls didn't swear.
In my time girls didn't have boyfriends.
In my time girls didn't smoke.
In my time...
Mama your time is over. Your time is history, antique. Set your watch right and get on with my time. And stop whining. But mama keeps re-

winding the tape in her mind and I've been hearing the same shit for years now. And the list goes on.

You can't have a real friendship with a boy.

Boys have tsootsoos and their tsootsoos get in the way.

Boys grow up to be the breadwinners. I guess it escapes her that bread isn't my favorite food.

Boys are boys. That's one of her deepest statements.

Boys need us. She likes to think that.

You can't go against nature. You are a girl. Girls don't pee standing. That's mama's mega joke so I am supposed to smile and agree menially.

Well mama! Try me. 'Cause it's two o'clock in the morning and I am standing in the middle of the school's backyard, legs shoulders-width apart, an *animal* hangs from my lower lip, my skirt is up and I am squeezing my stomach muscles and here it comes I am pissing standing. I am pissing standing. I am pissing against nature. I am pissing against mama. I am pissing off mama. And Antonis, Maria, and Bo are pissing next to me. We make art with our hot golden steams.

And as I am about to celebrate the piss-standing-victory Bo says, "In America cool dudes have one-night stands," and then he jerks it with both hands, making sure that the last drop doesn't reach his CK boxers.

"In Greece cool dudes don't follow any rules," Antonis replies zipping his up.

"My mama wasn't a virgin when she married my baba," I say and they all turn and look at me as if I've just made the most profound statement of all time. And then there is silence. Silence like the kind that makes your ears burn, the loudest type of all.

Silence.

Silence.

Silence.

No one is moving. They just stand there as if I've pushed the pause button. What the fuck is happening? I ask myself, and wanting to break the ice, I go on.

"She has been feeding me the wrong fairytale for years now. All her bullshit about how she loved only one man and how she's known only one hug and how she was the mega Virgin Mary of her time, it's all fucking bullshit. Mega fucking bullshit."

"How do you know?" Maria asks, when what I really want her to ask is: What does it matter?

"What difference does it make? I know. Everybody knows," I say and pull up my panties. I am wearing my pink coolest panties of all, the one with the red logo on my butt, kiss my ass. That was Antonis's and Maria's birthday present. They had to go all the way to Thessalonica to get me that. Sometimes you just need someone to kiss your ass, it's normal, cool, they said as I was staring at the logo, and then they squeezed me in their arms singing happy birthday in the Greek version. That was my last birthday. No candles. No nothing. Mama was still mourning baba's departure. It was just few months from the day he packed his things and went to live with his mama.

"So she wasn't a virgin. It doesn't mean shit," Antonis says and flips his zippo open, trying to light an *animal.*

"You damn well know what it can really mean," I yell and the loud tone of my voice surprises me.

"It means shit," Antonis insists once more, his voice already adapted to his loud tenacious tone. I know the tone; it's overprotective, stubborn, kind of cool if you are the one to generate it but in this case I am not. I am supposed to be listening. For one more time I am supposed to be swallowing his fabrications, swallowing everybody's fabrications, playing out the role of the wounded dumped kid. Well. Surprise! The play is over. No more mega shit. No more pretty fiction. No more perhaps and maybes.

"You know very well what it can mean, let's not throw away any more of our gray-matter recycling the same stuff over and over," I say in a lower tone.

"You need a cigarette?" Bo asks Maria.

"I need more than a cigarette," she replies, pulling up her jeans. She is a goddess, long lingering legs, tender lips, flat stomach, perfect ass. Where did she get all this? I wonder silently while the image of her old folks comes into my mind. How come some ugly decayed bodies like those can manufacture such sperm? Well, who can give an answer to that? Definitely not me. I don't even know the whereabouts of my own damn sperm.

"Even if she wasn't a virgin when she did it with your baba it doesn't mean what you are saying," Maria states slowly placing her butt on the floor, only a few steps away from our still-steaming art.

"But it CAN mean that. Can't it?" I say, parking next to her.

"It can mean many things," Antonis replies looking at Bo. Bo is in full silence. Simply staying out of it, silently reassuring me once more that he along with the rest of the village is well informed about the whole thing, fact which makes me the only fucking mega ignorant. I guess nowadays bad news travels at a greater speed than light. I am 100 percent sure that this information would have pissed off Einstein as much as it has pissed me off. Anyway, that's one more characteristic of my time. Information flows everywhere within micro-micro-micro-micro seconds. Nothing you can do to prevent the leakage. The whole world is working against you.

"What do you know?" I turn and ask Bo.

"About what?" he replies, puffing a smoke ring without making eye contact.

"Forget it, guys. Just consider yourselves my fucking enemies," I say in a pretty friendly tone and stand up ready to make my exit, but at that very moment Antonis comes closer and grabs my wrist.

"Let's not hit bottom. Melodramas and emotional bullshit aren't my type," I say and pull back.

"Let us tell you what we've heard," Antonis replies between puffs, gazing from me to the others.

So once again I park my butt on the dirt and, since I am promised the whole truth and nothing but the truth, I sit tight. A couple of minutes pass and a big silence settles on us for the second time. For a while everybody seems trapped inside their own heads. Then I see Bo taking a strong inhale from his Camel. He walks towards me with bloated cheeks and a sec later I feel his lips on top of mine. I know what I am supposed to do although this is the first time I am doing it. Sucking the warm smoke out of his mouth feels better than *jumping*. Then he sits next to me, pulls off the black ribbon which holds his long dark hair and starts like this:

"Once upon a time there was a girl..." His voice is hoarse but smooth, almost erotic. He isn't telling us about Little Red Riding Hood. He is telling us how much my mama loved my baba and what she went through to protect her love. The story is familiar; I've heard it before except for some micro details. For instance, how a lawyer from the capital stole mama's virginity a few days before her first night with baba. And ten minutes later the story comes to an end but the-live-happily-ever-after part is missing. I guess Bo knows only the adult's version, I think as I walk home wiping off my eye juices.

The Invention of GG

Mrs. Calliga places her right hand on her neck. Her throat feels dry, as if she had been gulping extra large pieces of lamb and it got scratched. But she hasn't had meat for more than a week now and she knows it. Unfortunately for her and fortunately for the lamb the throat dryness was caused by an ordinary plastic tube, which doctor Nikos pushed down her throat ten days ago when he laid her flat on the operating table, naked waist up, breasts hanging left to right. What a humiliating scene—and thinking about it doesn't make her feel any better. But there is nothing she can do. It's done. Happened in a great rush. Like a summer thunder or a nightmare that leaves you with dark circles under your eyes.

And it went like this: It was about an hour before the mega dinner, so Mrs. Calliga went up to her room to get dressed. She held her pretty dress with both hands low to her knees and raised one leg up then the other and there she was fully in. But when she reached for the zipper and tried to squeeze her double D tits into the light green silky fabric, she started suspecting that her boobs had expanded without further notice. Just like that. So she took a big inhale and tried once more. But in vain.

Sophia will do it, she thought and yelled, "Sophia, get in here. I need you."

Kyra Sophia untied her apron and in no time she was standing next to Mrs. Calliga.

"Can you please zip me up? I cannot seem to manage it by myself."

"No problem Missus," Kyra Sophia replied and dived into her duty.

She pulled from the left. Nothing. Then she pulled from the right. Nothing once more. So she pushed. A third nothing. Finally she pulled from the left and right and pushed all at once. But she came up with the last and biggest nothing of all. Nothing!

"Missus I can't seem to be able to get it. I'm missing about five centimeter …"

"For God's shake, what is going on?" Mrs. Calliga shouted in mega fumes.

"It might have shrunk. The fabric you know."

"No, I haven't washed it from the last time I wore it," Mrs. Calliga replied in low volume and skeptically added, "You know my breasts feel swollen. Actually my right one is a bit sour."

"Let me take a look my Missus," Kyra Sophia responded in her usual calm tone.

Kyra Sophia knew Mrs. Calliga upside down. She was Missus's nanny and carry nineteen years more than her. If something were wrong Kyra Sophia was able to spot it in seconds. And something was wrong.

"Oh!! My Missus, your breast is hard like a stone. Does it hurt?" she asked, squeezing Mrs. Calliga's right tit.

"No, not really. I just feel a pinch, a tiny little something," Mrs. Calliga replied in confusion.

"But this is not tiny. This is big and purple. You gotta show it to the ladies' doc."

"Yeah, yeah I will. But it's not time for that now. Get me my black dress, the one with the beads, you know. I am late. I have to get down," Mrs. Calliga uttered and ten minutes later she was standing next to her Master playing the role of the cheerful pleasant hostess.

The night came and left almost as planned. Rabbit and chicken were gone. About a third of the leg lamb was still around. The guest had more than a good appetite. He had a great one, leaving with an overstretched belly and a satisfied look but Mrs. Calliga was in troublesome mood. Actually she was pretty concerned. Concerned about her right tit and her youngest.

"What is it, my woman? You don't approve of the man?" the Master questioned, looking at her wrinkled sour face.

"No, no," she replied, rubbing her right tit in full circles, and exited the room.

So Monday morning came and the bad news arrived in passionate mystic tone.

"You have it—the devil's thing. How did it get to you, Mrs. Calliga? I really can't understand. And it's eating you from inside out. Tortuously. Eating you in a big hurry," Doctor Nikos eyed Mrs. Calliga through his thick glasses in full confusion.

"How did it get to you Mrs. Calliga? How?" He murmured a couple more times gripping Missus's breast with his baby fingers. He wasn't really waiting for an answer but kept asking, "How did it get to you? How?"

"Are you sure doc? Is that it? The devil's thing?" Missus whispered.

"Yes! As a scientist I am 100 percent sure but as a simple man I cannot comprehend it."

And it was true. Poor Doc Nikos couldn't understand how the bloody flesh eater got to a rich and respectable woman like Mrs. Calliga. For years now he had witnessed many cases but all of them were spread upon the low class people—people who made their entrance in this world with nothing, were destined to live with nothing, and died pretty much with less than nothing. And these people knew from the very start that sooner or later they would be eaten by one of the world's greatest monsters. Society or filthy nature would devour them with pleasure. So they were waiting reverentially for the bad thing to happen. They were waiting like a sinner waits to get his redemption. And in most cases when the devil's thing knocked on their doors they were relieved 'cause they knew that it arrived only to save them from the next worst thing. But this? This was beyond comprehension. Mrs. Calliga wasn't one of those. Mrs. Calliga had nothing to do with those low-class filthy creatures. Mrs. Calliga had money, respect and a first class name. Mrs. Calliga wasn't to be treated like that. And that's why doctor Nikos was in full awe. Shocked. Almost unable to converse.

"There must be a mistake. These things don't happen to people like us. Right Doc? Right?" Missus said as if she had been reading his thoughts.

"We… we… we will fight it Mrs. Calliga," doctor Nikos finally managed to say. Then he took a deep breath, put on his revenge face, straightened up his bow tie and went on, "Don't worry about it. We'll destroy the bloody thing. I give you my word."

And it happened as he said. The next day Mrs. Calliga woke up in a bright blue nightgown with TH (Thessalonici Hospital) initials on her sleeve and her right tit missing. Gone! Forever and ever! So? She was minus one double-D tit. No big deal. Right? And the answer is: Wrong! TOTALLY WRONG! In mega capitals. 'Cause missing a double-D tit is nothing like missing an A, B or even a C cup tit. When you are missing a double-D tit it's like landing on an over-flat valley after living for forty-two years in the Alps. So at that very desperate moment Mrs. Calliga realized that she needed something greater than life. And what's greater than life? That's an easy one. GG.

Great God was, is, and will be greater than life. From that moment on Mrs. Calliga was a bit less than Mrs. Calliga, don't forget she was minus four kilos, that's the estimated weight of her right double-D tit, but her simple God became Great God and that filled her up. Filled her up with faith. Fat mega faith piled up inside Mrs. Calliga. But outside she was still a tit less. So she asked doctor Nikos, "Is there something we can do to cover it up?"

"Well, let's worry about that when you have fully recovered," doctor Nikos replied and patted her on the shoulder.

"Science cannot do much. Can it?" she said, more to herself than to the doctor, and closed her eyes pleading in desperate twos (GG-GG, GG-GG) for Divine help. And she was right 'cause it's common knowledge by now that GG is not a magician, so swinging His stick and getting back your missing tit is out of the question, but He is a great redeemer and redemption instead of magic is like having sex instead of masturbating so she went straight for the real stuff like any other normal human being would have.

"You just don't worry. Relax and I am sure we'll do something about that," doctor Nikos said, trying to comfort her, but Mrs. Calliga was mentally far away, picking up a full bag of devotion and running to catch up with life, which had been rolling all this time without her.

On the Road to the Magic Bra

Too much estrogen, and you get bitch tits.
—Chuck Palahniuk, *Fight Club*

So once again Mrs. Calliga places her right hand on her neck. Her throat feels dry. Now we know why. It is the tenth day after the operation. GG is around 100 percent and devotion is in the air. Right double-D tit is still missing but cheesecloth fills up its empty flat spot, and like all girls who go around proud showing off their wonder-bra tits living in the illusion that faking it is as good as having the real thing, so with similar spirits Mrs. Calliga goes around the Calliga Mansion, getting ready for the mega event. In a week's time her youngest is getting married and single-tit mama is determined to look her best.

So she orders new table cloths, new matching curtains, new rugs, new sleepers, new silverware, new panties, new china coffee cups, new that and new this. And most important of all she orders the best seamstress in town, Madam Papadimou, to visit the mansion in deep darkness. When everybody is in bed. 100% asleep. Because Mrs. Calliga has decided to give Madam Papadimou the honor to create her magic bra. The one which she will be wearing under her pretty velvet dress at her youngest's wedding. The one with the stuffed right cup. The one which if girls had known about in those days they would have married better.

Of course Madam Papadimou is to keep the whole thing buried deep inside her. The world needs to know nothing about operations, missing tits and magic bras. The world needs to keep up its pretty round image so Madam Papadimou is asked to swear to Great God for eternal silence.

"But of course Mrs. Calliga. I will say nothing to no one. My lips are sealed," Madam Papadimou swears, holding her right hand up pretending to touch an invisible Bible while her eyes expand beyond limits staring at Mrs. Calliga's missing tit.

"GG only knows how things like these happen to us," Mrs. mumbles.

"G?G? Yeah G G !" Madam Papadimou repeats without knowing what she is really saying, eyes still nailed on big flat nothing.

After a brief summary of the story Madam Papadimou learns all about the operation and the missing tit. So her eyes are back to their usual size and now her creativity is in full function.

"Don't worry, my Missus. I'll make you a new one in less than a day. It'll be better than the real thing. Even gravity will be scared away. Even gravity."

"Well, I only want to look good for my daughter. No one else, only for my Chrysa," Mrs. Calliga replies, standing still as Madam takes her measures.

"What a mama can do for her child only Virgin Mary knows." Madam jerks her head in full agreement but a minute later her face changes. She takes a few steps away from Mrs. Calliga and stares at her tentatively.

"What is it? It won't work?" Mrs. Calliga asks in great anxiety.

"No nothing like that but...but... well I thought of something."

"Well, go on then," Mrs. Calliga encourages Madam Papadimou.

"You know Puta. Don't you? Soto's child. That... that...weird kind of fellow."

"Of course I do. I mean I've seen him around. You know it's not in our class to socialize with these kinds of people. They are nobodies, if you know what I mean," Mrs. Calliga says taking a proud inhale, nose pointing to the mega sky, nostrils wide open in full operation.

"Well, do you know what people say?" and without waiting, "he doesn't have his big tits from God. No! No! God has nothing to do with his mega tits. Actually he went to a doc in Thessalonici who gave him some pills and in a day or so he was full of breasts. So I thought maybe... maybe..."

"Well tits aren't like lizards' tails, tits don't grow back like that. Right?" Mrs. Calliga states, trying to keep her voice in neutral mode.

"I'm telling you I've seen them with my own eyes," Madam adds and then looking around making sure no one is listening she comes closer to Mrs. Calliga and continues, "Don't say this to anyone but ... but you know how I know?" And without waiting, "Well, I am the one who makes his shirts. He can't get into a real man's shirts so his mama calls me twice a year and I sew all the shirts for him. That's how I come to know such a private thing. I've seen them. They are big like balloons and real, 100 percent real. As far as I know those aren't man's tits. I have raised four daughters; my oldest one is twenty-four. I've seen hundreds of ladies. And God is not playing with things like that. Only science. Only science is responsible for such abnormalities," Madam goes on and on and Mrs. Calliga is now in full attention. Her eyes stretch beyond their limits. Her heartbeat is reaching peaks. If she were able to get a couple of those pills, everything would be normal once again. But how can you ask for such a favor? Is it moral? If GG decides to take a piece of you, is it right to go behind His back? Is it science or the devil's game? Mrs. Calliga is in deep dilemma; her single tit is bouncing up and down, her face is flushing, her palms are moist.

"Mrs. Calliga, are you alright? Mrs. Calliga?" Madam Papadimou questions staring in blank confusion.

"I...I am okay," Mrs. Calliga manages to say between deep inhales. "I guess I am still weak from the operation. I might sit down for a minute," she says and reaches for the chair behind her.

"Please do take your time. I can come back tomorrow night if you like. It's not a big bother for me. It's my job. I can come back anytime," Madam replies and starts putting her needles and pins inside her little sewing box, still eyeing Missus with mega perplexity.

"Yes. That would be better. Let's do this tomorrow. Same time," Mrs. Calliga says while one hand holds her heavy head and the other the missing tit.

A Long Night

That night Mrs. Calliga wasn't able to doze off even for a single minute. She turned and twisted and turned and twisted. Over and over. Again and again. Good thing she wasn't sleeping in the same bed with the Master. You see after the operation the Master had ordered Kyra Sophia to set up the main guest room for his wife—for extra comfort, he said, but he was really afraid that he might catch the disease. The mayor had told him that a friend of a friend had got a similar disease by sleeping with a low man in the capital, so the Master decided to play it safe and keep away until his wife was 100 percent cured. Furthermore, the main guest room was next to Kyra Sophia's bedroom, *an ideal arrangement* for both women, the Master suggested. Mrs. Calliga agreed happily, thinking that finally GG had freed her from her husband's dirty sexual habits once and for all.

So while Mrs. Calliga was stretching her wounded body in all directions trying to find the best position to catch some z's, her mind was racing. She replayed in her head about fifty more times the conversation she had with Madam Papadimou. Once she was over with that, her imagination went on, flying in pleasant colorful skies. She saw Fucking Auntie Puta with his big tits standing in full erection, next to him there were pills, many pills in all shapes, sizes and colors. No. No. This wasn't a dream. Mrs. Calliga hadn't even reached her first sleeping cycle so she was nowhere near her REM department. On the contrary, she was fully awake, soaked in her own sweat, eyes wide open. If only she were able to get her tit back. Just for a day. Just for Chrysa's wedding. How wrong would that be? Only a day and then she would happily give it back. But how would she manage such a thing without asking Fucking Auntie Puta? Would she be able to ask Madam Papadimou for help without damaging the family name? Woulds and hows were keeping her mind fully occupied while Puta's tits and jelly multicolored pills were keeping her eyes active. She felt overloaded, exhausted.

"GG! GG!" she yelled a couple of times, inhaling with great effort, but it was GG's night off. "My GG!" she shouted once more but nothing. Then she stood up on her bed, shut her eyes tightly, squeezing Fucking Auntie Puta out of them and pleaded, "Sophia! Kyra Sophia! Please!" And the miracle happened. In no time Kyra Sophia was standing next to her holding a glass of water in her hand.

In the mean time, at the other end of the village Madam Papadimou's fingers were in full action, dialing numbers one after another. First Madam Papadimou called Pauper's neighbor, that's Pauper's mama's official girlfriend, otherwise known as Fragile, a nickname awarded to her by her deceased husband at the first month of their wedding. A nickname that fitted her much better than her given birth name, Sotiria, which means Salvation in the official English translation. And before going on to explain the reasons for Madam Papadimou's phone calls let's talk a bit about Sotiria, Salvation or simply Fragile, as most call her. We'll start with the obvious: Fragile was fragile. She possessed two elastic sticks for legs, an over-whining voice functioning in low volume at all times, 4,663 freckles covering her smooth milky epidermis and a lot of patchouli, her prime time aroma as she liked to call it. Fragile's house was opposite to Pauper's. Fragile's husband, as it was mentioned, had gone to the heavens about ten years earlier in the middle of a heavy winter, leaving Fragile cold, alone and unguarded. So Pauper's mama, who was known for her mega strong heart, ran to comfort her neighbor. She opened her arms, squeezed Fragile against her warm chest and with her lips she started wiping the tears off her crowded-freckled face. The first minute Fragile felt confusion, but ten minutes later affection came along and confusion was gone forever. After that things were easy. Fragile started sharing her thoughts, her telephone (note that Pauper's house was short of such luxuries), her bed and her panties with Pauper's mama. Everyone got a whiff of the news in the village but in those times affection without tsootsoos wasn't a dangerous matter. Of course it was a sin but it was a white sin and white sins are like white lies, they come and go without mega damage.

So Madam Papadimou dialed Fragile's number with the hope of finding Pauper's mama there but Pauper's mama was elsewhere. Where was she? Well based on what has been said by now a pretty logical guess would be that she was pulling her husband out of the famous dry ditch. But she wasn't. Why? Simply because her husband and my almost-drunk-pappoo-to-be was totally dead and flying in the great blue skies along with Mrs. Calliga's left tit. Of course this is pretty lethal headline news but be patient, a full layout of the deadly event will be coming soon. For now let's just imagine Pauper's mama as a freshly mega widow, sitting on one of the stools at Paradise with the Key-holder and the rest of the boys, gulping some ouzo shots and trying to ease up her wounded heart. And at the other end of the stage once again was Madam Papadimou who for the second time put her fingers in action dialing the number at Paradise. Then one, two, three, four. "Ring! Ring!" And bingo! The person in question was found.

"Those things shouldn't go through telephone lines. I gotta see you face to face. I am telling you it's for your son's good. Otherwise you would find me in bed by now," Madam Papadimou's anxious voice traveled through the rusty telephone line. And at the other end of the hook Pauper's mama was pushing the receiver on her left ear with her right hand, playing her amber worry beads with the left while holding her breath trying to stop the damn annoying hiccup that arrived from nowhere after the first round of ouzo shots. Note here that Pauper's mama was in a pretty uncomfortable position and the boys' giggles didn't help much. So she yelled, "What?" and then "Who?" and finally "Yeah, yeah. If you say so. I'll be there in a few." Then she hung the receiver on the hook, she swung her worry beads around a couple of times, bolted a second ouzo shot, tied her funeral veil over her gray hair, and exited Paradise with heavy steps.

Meanwhile Madam Papadimou's fingers were going through a third set of numbers. This time Fucking Auntie Puta's phone was ringing.

And his mama, Kyra Soto, all wrinkled up, got off her pillow and looked around in total disorientation.

"The phone. It's the phone," she finally said, and rushed to it and then, "At this hour?"

(...)

"She is coming too?"

(...)

"Well, I'd better hurry then."

She put down the receiver, got out of her nightgown, got into her brown everyday dress and headed for Madam Papadimou's.

Deadly News (Wednesday, September 4, 1963)

Â nd now let's go a bit farther back for the full layout of the deadly event as promised.

Five hours had passed from the time Kyra Sophia had delivered Chrysa's love letter to our hero. And yes! He was in full delirium. Totally content. Ready to die for love or from love. Anyway it wasn't time for such micro details; now had to write! Write his first love letter, promise his eternal loyalty. It wasn't like he had an option or something. Kyra Sophia was coming next day for the reply and until then he had to find the proper words. Pretty words, words suitable for virgin chicks, poetic words, words for mega romantic lovers like himself. But where do you find such words? Word-malls weren't invented yet and he hadn't the luxury of waiting forever. So he murmured, "Fucking gray balls," and then, "now that I need Dimitris, now he isn't talking to me." And he walked back and forth, back and forth, holding Chrysa's note in his hands and puffing like an old electric tram.

"Bloody hell, I gotta do something about this," he yelled to himself making a fist and grinding his teeth with anger. And two seconds later, "My Britannica, my Britannica. That will save me!" he screamed in mega ecstasy. He kneeled under the bed in a great rush and a few minutes later he was holding all five volumes of the Britannica encyclopedia in his hands. Without opening them he took a good look at each one. There was K, L, O, some of E and most of F and the whole of V.

What a treasure I've got, he thought to himself releasing a big toothless smile. *I am an educated man. One day I am going to read all of them, hide my nose deep inside them and come out only when I am done. One day*

I am going to be a rich man. My head will be stuffed with letters, my mouth with new fancy words, my heart...well my heart...

And while he was stretching his mental cords to their limits, suddenly the door slammed wide open. In less than a sec the whole room was swamped in patchouli. What a smell! Pauper's nostrils pumped up with cheap aroma. His mama was standing in front of him, hands on her waist, mouth opened, eyes half shut, gazing in total confusion.

"What the hell are you doing on the floor with all those books on top of you? Have you lost it?" she asked stepping forward and immediately added, "Well I forget. You gotta have it first in order to lose it and if I judge from your latest behavior you haven't got any." And a big sarcastic laugh filled the room, "Haaa! Haaa! Haaa!"

"Mama your whining genes are winning you over," Pauper replied, standing up slowly. "Anyway, what did you fall in? All that stink!" And without waiting, "Don't even bother, I might not have a brain but I don't need a brain to answer that question. Everybody knows that. Even loonies know about your unique taste. Kyra Vana with the Big Balls! That's your nickname. Isn't it?"

"Someone has to wear the balls in this family. And since you and your baba don't bother...anyway leave my balls aside and tell me what's all this? The toilet paper isn't good enough for you?" Kyra Vana questioned, eyeing the books with a mocking gaze.

"Mama this is Britannica. This is the best encyclopedia in the whole world. This is a mega treasure."

"And why have you decided to open up your mega treasure today my son?" she asked ironically, eyebrows fully arched, stroking her worry beats with her right hand.

"I need to write something and I wanna get the right words," Pauper replied seriously.

"Why don't you use your mouth if you wanna say something? Why waste ink and paper? What's so important?" she asked in one breath still holding the ironic tone.

But Pauper said nothing. He just looked around and around without focusing. Anyway, Kyra Vana didn't need more to start off one of her famous lectures. She only needed a tiny little hint of brain fuzziness and then she was able to go on and on for hours. She was one of the best talkers in the whole village. She knew it, Pauper knew it, and everybody else knew it. She simply possessed the best vocab of all time. No funky bullshit with cheap wrapping but frank, straightforward words with full meaning and top value. So she went on:

"Let's say you wanna write your will or something, why don't you go to Dimitris's then? He is the mega pencil pusher, isn't he? The impromptu poet, the sweet talker, the smooth paper soul. And now let me tell you why you don't go to Dimitris's. 'Cause you don't possess the balls for such a sacred act. And I am telling you once and for all friendship is the only thing worth living for in this world. Friendship is the only religion left worth believing in. Friendship is what we got after Eve ate the apple. Friendship is bigger than God. Friendship was, is and will be the only cosmic good karma that holds this shitty world in order. And now let me tell you one more thing; decent people believe in friendship. Decent people don't dump their friends for pretty eyes. Decent people sacrifice their lives for their friends. In simple words, decent people and most specifically *real men* think with their upper head, not with the lower. So I am telling you for the thousandth time go and ask Dimitris for forgiveness before it's too late and leave your big treasures for later."

The truth was that Pauper agreed 100 percent with his mama; that's why he was listening without making a sound. Just looking stoically while keeping his hands occupied placing some of E plus most of F on top of K on top of L on top of O on top of V and feeling extra guilty for spoiling the only first rate relationship he ever had. Deep inside he wanted to do the right thing but something was holding him back, and as long as he wasn't able to label that something, he wasn't going anywhere. What was that something? Well, it felt like an itching tumor growing underneath the base of his heart but he knew that sometimes it's not worth tracing tumors to their roots so he decided to be patient and let time work its magic. Of course time had a different opinion on this one. So at that very moment a heavy abrupt knock (knock-knock) shook the front door and in no time mama and son put on their unpleasant faces and questioned with one voice, "Who is that?"

Their reaction was totally justified. It was 3 o'clock in the afternoon, siesta time and during siesta time the whole village was in deep sleep. But there was no second round of knocks to let mama and son fabricate a single thought, just a big slam on the door and there was Dimitris in full upheaval, burning cheeks and puffing breaths in mega rush.

"Your baba, your baba is at the clinic. I found him outside Paradise. He is very sick, he... he...he couldn't breath," he said, spitting all over Pauper's face.

"There is more than one word for that, it's called drunkenness or ouzoness or ..." Kyra Vana said in low voice.

"No. No. This is serious. You gotta come to the clinic now," Dimitris insisted still eyeing at Pauper, sending him a mystic but clearly sad message. Pauper got the message in less than a sec, so he put on his black pants, his white shirt and headed for the clinic, following Dimitris in full silence.

Ten minutes later he arrived at the clinic but his baba's spirit wasn't there, it was gone, reaching great blue skies. Without knowing what he was supposed to do, he just stood there, eyes nailed on the happy over-flushed corpse's face. In the air there was a pretty familiar smell. Ouzo! Ouzo! And more ouzo! Pauper inhaled deeply with great effort as if he wanted to suck in the entire air of the room. About two to three minutes later he felt dizzy, so he adapted to normal inhaling/exhaling levels, squeezed some juices out of his eyes, trying to think what to do next.

It was then he remembered that all this time his old pal Dimitris was standing behind him in pause mode. So Pauper opened his eyes, wiped the juices off his cheeks, turned around and looked at Dimitris straight in the eye. It was as if friendship was staring over death. And what happens when friendship stares at death? Well that's like asking what's Mega Alexander's first name. It prevailed. Friendship stood imperiously over death and Dimitris found himself in the arms of Pauper. Or was it the other way around? Anyway the two friends hugged and hugged and hugged while mini nurse Margarita was running around the village delivering the deadly news.

Current Era

Jumpers & Lovers/Fuckers

When did I decide to stop *jumping* George? (The blank space below serves like an eye-rest; vision-vacation type of exercise, so you don't go on to the next line without giving it a thought).

S

O

T

H

I

N

K

Now once again. When did I decide to stop *jumping* George? If you thought that I decided to stop *jumping* George when I started *jumping* Bo, you thought completely wrong and totally identically with Maria. The true, genuine answer is this: I decided to stop *jumping* George when I found out that he paid 32,568 drachmas, (about seventy to eighty bucks) to buy a blue color pen, which was claimed to write upside-down without gaps. And now if you wonder why, I have a pretty simple explanation. It goes like this. I refuse to *jump*, support or be a part of such great levels of thickness. In other words, why would you spend that kind of money when you can get the same affect out of a five-drachma pencil? Well, I can think of several reasons but they are all dull, dumb, and dim. And believe me, quitting George-*jumping* wasn't an easy decision. On the contrary, it was a pretty tricky and difficult one since I was putting my Semi-Annual Jumper's (SAJ) score at great risk, losing points day in and day out. But before going on to personal inevitabilities let's get the SAJ facts straight. First of all, how do you get to be a winner of the SAJ medal? Well, that's simple math. The more *jumps* you score the more points you accumulate. For instance, the previous Semi-Annual Jumper's medal for the first six months of that year (January to June, total number of days: 181) was awarded to Antonis, who managed to accumulate ninety-four *jumps*. No. Two was George with sixty-eight points, one more and he would have given a totally different meaning to the whole score. Note here that at that time George was full-time *jumping* a pretty ugly and stupid chick while I was in deep dilemma—to *jump* or not to *jump* him—since he was a friend and it's only decent to avoid *jumping* friends. No. Three was me with fifty-six points, half of which were scored at Loo's WC in mega great rush, less than a five minute operation (luckily for me chrono-geographic details don't affect SAJ's numbers). Last but coolest was Maria with forty-four *jumps* and the highest Semi-Annual Variety (SAV) score of thirteen, meaning that she had managed to perform her forty-four *jumps* with thirteen different victims, that's 3.38 *jumps* per person. Of course it must be said once more that Maria possesses the longest, prettiest legs in the whole universe and the wildest, juiciest lips in the entire solar system, so picking out the *jumping* victims of her choice isn't a difficult task, although we should keep in mind that good supply is always an issue since finding someone who is better-than-average is like going to the corner deli to buy gourmet food. But Maria is an open-minded food taster; in other words, she isn't a leftover eater. She would rather have a fresh can of spaghetti and cheese than yesterday's fillet mignon. Well, Maria is Maria and her *jumping* methods aren't for everybody. Also, explanations like the 32,568 drachmas upside-down-pens don't make a lot of sense to Maria so here I am once again at Loo's going over the same stuff, trying to explain to her that I decided to quit *jumping* George 'cause his actions are against my values, morals, ethics et cetera et cetera and not because I had an appetite for a well-done New York sirloin.

So for the twentieth time she asks, "Why the fuck do you care if George wants to spend his money on upside-down pens?"

"It's a matter of ethics. I don't *jump* empty heads. My parking is for high class engines," I reply in indignation.

"Honey you make no sense. *Jumping* is *jumping* and has nothing to do with Spinoza, Kant and the rest of the boys. Once and for all, get it right, *jumping* is based on the simplest physical law of ins and outs and lasts as long as you do it. Loving-slash-fucking is based on emotional and ethical bullshit and—surprise, surprise—this year it's out of fashion. Got it?"

I nod, praying silently for an epiphany shock, but it doesn't seem to be my lucky day. So I see Maria getting ready to perform her famous speech. She slips into her funky Miss Universe look, licks her succulent lips a couple of times, and starts:

"You know, babe, the world is divided into two mega categories: *jumpers* and lovers slash fuckers. Note here that the latter group starts always as lovers and ends up always as fuckers. But let's start with those that come first, the *jumpers*. The *jumpers* are the honest, the good type, the clear-cut brand. Those are the ones who ask for your permission before they go on to *jump* you and if you say no they get on with their life and you get on with yours. No hard feelings. Those are the ones who keep their physical needs separate from their emotional craves. Those are the ones who do it for the sake of doing it. In other words, love, fidelity, long plans, marriage and prosperity don't get in their way. So those give you no emotional traumas, only erotic bruises that you don't bother covering up. Anyway, why would you?

She pauses, blowing at my face smoothly, coolly with charm and buoyancy. When she is done blowing, she thrusts her pointer into her mouth and pops out her cheek.

"Pop pop and pop pop."

That's her way of telling me, *wake up, girl, wake up*, but I look at her with indifference. Once she realizes that I am not going to reply she stops the popping, sucks her finger and goes on.

"So I repeat, why don't you bother covering up your erotic bruises after a *jump*, babe? You know why or do I have to spell everything out for you?"

At this point she gives me no time to reply. Quickly she readjusts her butt on the stool and goes on.

"Well, babe, I have given you the answer already but let me repeat it. When there are no emotional traumas involved, or any type of feelings for that matter, why would you bother covering up your erotic bruises?"

"'Cause you don't want your private business becoming everybody else's business, that's why, that's why you cover up your hickeys," I say, pulling back my whole torso trying to be out of breath's reach.

"Oh girl, you break my heart now," she shouts and her whole face changes from diva's to joker's. I say nothing, just look at her. She forces a dry laugh while she sends me a pitiful look. Then she shakes her head a couple of times as if she wants to reload her thoughts and continues.

"So let's start once again 'cause I think I haven't made it clear what makes a *jumper* a *jumper* and a fucker a fucker simply 'cause I hadn't had the chance to go on to the second category. So let me give it a second try. As I said, *jumpers* are the clear-cut type, they *jump*, in other words have sex and that's it. Feelings, commitments et cetera et cetera are all out of the game. Right?" she asks and I nod 'cause I know that any objections would cause me infinite hours of arguing. So she continues.

"Now the second type, lovers/fuckers or love-makers as most call them, are the evil, the psycho-pathetic brand. Those are the ones who fuck you without asking, just to boost up their egos. Simply mega egocentrics if you ask me. Those are like cockroaches. They move into your apartment without any intention of paying rent and talk about ethics, love, rights and wrongs just because they want to justify their fucking impulses. Those are like cancer, wanna stick around forever. They use their tsootsoos in order to poison your brain and wound your heart. And let me make it clear here that when I say their tsootsoos I speak for both sides, men and women. Don't think that just because women have no tsootsoos they are incapable of fucking. Let me tell you, in this society women end up doing the most fucking. So as you understand fucking has less to do with the actual act and more to do with emotional poisoning. And as far as emotional business goes, women are the bosses here. Of course I am talking about the every day female type, the *small* feminine women who talk about feminism and equality but at the same time play the fragile female victim roles to their best. But let's not get out of our theme here. So in conclusion, *jumpers* *jump*, and fuckers fuck. Can't be clearer than that. Can it?" she asks with mega enthusiasm and great satisfaction. Then there is a two-second pause while she inhales deeply, making sure that I got the info straight, and then the exhale comes and she is on to her final set of questions.

"So now you got it right, how is it with Bo? Is he better than George or what?"

"I've done nothing with Bo," I say, pretty pissed off.

"So how is nothing? Bigger? Harder?"

"Cut it out. I am not in the mood. And just for your record I am planning to hibernate for the next couple of months. Get rusted. Live like Mary the Virgin if you know what I mean," I say in a harsh tone.

Maria turns to my side, giving me the impression that she is swallowing an extra dry piece of shit, and, as soon as she is done swallowing, she pats me on the back adding, "You better be careful girl, she is the one who got pregnant."

Ancient Era

Olga-A Feminine Feminist Fan

Based on a verbal copy of the daily gossip *Hello-Maga-zine* of September 7, 1963, three days after Pauper's baba's death, Olga, Pauper's only and older sister from America, arrived in Greece in an extra stretched-out jersey black suit and a big matching sombrero. Her baba's body? Still around, waiting in the middle of the single room house. His ouzo aroma? Almost gone. His rosy cheeks? Sagged inside his broad cheekbones. His epidermis? Hung heavily over his decayed bones aiming for holy abysses but only reaching the itchy sides of a cardboard box, which was supposed to serve as a casket. And there was Olga, Pauper's dearest sister from America, standing in front of her baba's body, stretching her eyes in all directions, unable to believe what she was seeing.

"My baba. My baba," she gushed, sniffing in tiny weeps. "My baba. My baaa..." and pluuuffff she collapsed on top of Fragile who had happened to stand behind her. Fragile, being fragile and all, failed to hold on to Olga's extra kilos, so they both crashed down in the middle of the room, one on top of the other.

"Damn it," Kyra Vana hissed, "what a ridicule. More than a decade and she hasn't changed a bit. Ftoo! Ftoo!" she spat under her shoulder and added, "Little filthy womanly caprices for nothing."

Clearly enough mama and daughter weren't the best of friends. Olga was nothing like her mama. Olga possessed long ivory plastic manicured nails, penciled curvy lines for eyebrows, push up bras, lacy stockings, cherry lipsticks, black, green and brown mascaras, pink silky handkerchiefs, black, white and beige corsets, babyish frivolous vocal tunes in sweet low volumes and nine mini bottles of Chanel No. 5. Olga hid a mega wound between her legs, a smooth aroma between her boobs and a lot of elegance between her thoughts. Olga wasn't named the Queen of Femininity for nothing. Olga was femininity in its greatest glory. She knew how a woman was supposed to act, talk, walk and she followed the rules to her best. She was gone for eleven years and felt as if she hadn't seen her brothers forever, her baba for a couple of months and her mama for less than a day.

As far as Pauper was concerned, Olga was a glorious photo figure. He only knew her through three glamorous snaps she had sent him over the years. In the first she was standing underneath the statue of liberty wearing a white flair dress and a red rose squeezed between a succulent pair of tits. In the second she was standing on top of the Empire State Building in pink from head to toe, pumps included, hair poking out in every direction, (*Too much wind,* she wrote on the back). And in the third she was next to a flashing billboard in Times Square in white-blue, the national colors (the note said, *After attending the Greek Parade on the 25th of March*). In all three pictures she looked as if she was flowing in a mysterious luminous bubble, puffed-up with high pride and injected with many kilos of self-confidence. Clearly enough, like any other immigrant on Columbus's land, Olga had been fed the same old fairytale, hoping to hit the American dream any minute now. Of course, Pauper after studying and re-studying the pictures, came up with a pretty different theory. For Pauper and for any young naïve brother who is left behind believing that in America money grows on trees, Olga was the mega success, overloaded with green paper and glorious fame. Obviously Kyra Vana had a few objections over her son's theory but she was also a simple mama and like every simple mama she didn't want to ruin her son's feelings, so she left him to believe whatever damn well he pleased. After all Pauper had concrete solid evidence of his sister's mega success: the pictures and a golden Rolex made in China, a gift from his sister for his twenty-fifth birthday. Of course on September 7th, '63 Pauper had the opportunity to compare the real thing with the theory and surprisingly enough the real thing was proven better, greater, simply superior. How did it happen? Well, well, let's start from the beginning.

The day Olga arrived in Greece and precisely three days after her baba's death, Chrysa wrote her second love letter to Pauper. And she wrote love letter No. Two simply because a couple of days earlier she had received

Pauper's official love letter No. One. So once again Chrysa picked up her pen and along with her eternal loyalty and deepest sympathy squeezed a few warning sentences describing her huge concern about the upcoming mega dinner her parents were planning for her in a couple of days. Furthermore influenced by the latest deadly atmosphere, Chrysa went on to add the following pretty dramatic *P.S.: I'd rather die than find myself in the arms of another.* So when Chrysa's love-letter No. Two reached Pauper, Pauper did exactly was he was expected to do; smiled secretly (clearly he wasn't entitled to mega grins, let's not forger that his baba's corpse was resting next to him), then he opened the envelope and went on reading.

By the end of the last line he was fuming from all facial holes; ears, nostrils et cetera, et cetera. Olga who had arrived a couple of hours earlier viewed the scene from the edges of her pretty eyes while laying on the bed where she was placed to rest after the faint scene. First she saw her brother walking nervously around his baba a couple of times with the note in his hand and blasphemies between his grinding teeth. Then she saw him staring at the note for a couple of minutes mumbling in angry trios, *Damn it, damn it, damn it.* And suddenly and without premonition the view was distracted. She couldn't see a thing. You see Pauper parked his butt at the other end of the room on the loveseat just like that, without notice, so poor Olga lost full reception. If she wanted to watch the rest of the episode she had to act immediately, thus, she did. She stretched her body then rubbed her eyes with both hands as if she was just coming out of a deep sleep and asked in a smooth sweet tone, "What is it my brother?"

"Nothing, nothing," Pauper replied nervously trying to hide the letter in his pocket.

"Ops! Ups! Ops! Ups!" Olga moaned sitting up and then, "Forgive me but I've gathered a vast bag of experiences over the years and although I am in a pretty emotional state right now I can still sense that something is bothering you. And as a sensitive woman I can tell you that THAT something has nothing to do with baba's death. It has a rather different nature. Heart breaking? Romantic? Emotional? Perhaps deeply personal?"

It was weird, odd, strange, pretty bizarre to hear Olga's words. She wasn't just talking. She was mincing words. Her whole body was trembling with each word. Her eyelids were blinking in even rhythmical tempos. Her hands were floating in front of her deep V-neck. Her toes were in perfect Pointe. And those initial squeaky exclamations of hers. What were those? Were those for real?

When Pauper heard and saw all this he felt as if he were dreaming in someone else's head or maybe like walking on far foreign lands. Or was it more like having a brain cramp? Anyway one thing was certain, he never felt like this before. This was a prime, mega, major, first time experience leaving him incapable of fabricating any words or actions. But for Olga all this was a normal, everyday kind of thing. So she got up, walked slowly around her baba's body, discharging a long over-stretched ooofff, then inhaled deeply and after many micro-steps she stood beside her brother rubbing his shoulders with both hands.

"Ooff, ooff, my brother we are orphans, but at least we have each other." At that very minute Pauper's brain snapped out of it giving him a very unpredictable order. His right hand pulled out of his pocket Chrysa's love-letter No. Two and handed it to Olga. And BINGO! Three minutes later, that's how long it took Olga to read it, clearly her Greek was a little rusty, Olga went on rehearsing a monologue in huge excitement and mega honor. It was something like this.

"Oh my lord. It's so so romantic. You have to rescue the poor girl. It's a matter of pride. Times call for the survival of love. Nowadays people fight for their love. A woman's body can be subjugated but her heart never. I might still be single but I know about these things. I am a woman and I can sense a feminine heart in pain. I am a feminine soul myself."

"But how? What...what can I do?" Pauper murmured between Olga's ongoing paralogism.

But Queen Femininity had no intention of slowing down her verbal squeaks. "Oh! Oh! The poor little girl. Oh! Oh! You know I am feminine but I am also a big feminist believer. A Feminine Feminist Fan, these are my three mega F's one next to the other. F-F-F. My three mega ..." and at that point Olga was cut off by Fragile and Kyra Vana who walked in one behind the other with heavy determined steps.

"What's...what's...feminist?" Fragile asked warily.

"Pardon me?" Olga said, coming out of her mental blur.

"What's fe-me-nii-stt?" Fragile repeated stretching her lips beyond normal.

"Feminist is a woman who believes in feminism," Olga replied with pride while scrunching Chrysa's love letter between her fingers.

"And what's feminism?" asked Fragile once again.

"Feminism is when a woman is on top of a man," said Olga.

"My deceased used to call that easy-ride. You know, no sweat, no nothing," Fragile said gazing semi-shyly semi-slyly from Olga to Kyra Vana and vise versa.

Olga took out one of her pink silky handkerchiefs, sent a meaningful look to her brother, a sympathetic gaze to Fragile and exited the room seeking a gasp of fresh air. Pauper stood up and followed his sister in extra lethargic mode.

For Love's Sake

What is temperature wise boiling hot, color wise velvety red, size wise infinitely massive?

And

the

answer

is…

LOVE!

Love is boiling hot, velvety red and infinitely massive. Love paralyzes your mental cords, your logic, your common sense. Of course you know that and so does Olga. After all Olga was a mega romance reader devouring weekly at least 200 pages of cheap novellas, which she borrowed from her dearest and only friend in America, Betty Mulatto, a chocolate thin and tall beauty in red gypsy skirts, matching lipstick and charismatic voice. Thus, as a romantic expert Olga possessed a detailed bibliographical experience concerning all love matters, gone almost all the way through, reaching Ph.D. levels. So while she was outside her homestead, holding with one hand Chrysa's love letter No. Two, and with the other her pink handkerchief she started thinking that it was about time to put all her knowledge into practice, wrap up all theory models and go on to the real life experiment. As lingering minutes were pushing life forward, Olga's mind was slowly coming to a full stop, letting her heart take over. Once again she started making her micro-steps, this time in circular form, going around and around her brother who was still in deep mental narcosis. After completing circle No. Six, her heart was in full function, her brain in total halt: she was feeling dizzy but at the same time touched, moved, stirred, simply super ecstatic finally knowing what was her purpose at this page of her existence. So she stood on her toes and whispered in her brother's ear, "You'll take her."

"What!?" Pauper said, totally disoriented.

"You will take her," Olga repeated at half the speed.

"To where?"

"To your arms. Make her yours forever and ever," said Olga.

"You mean steeeaalll her?" Pauper asked while his eyes stretched to their maximum.

"There is nothing to steal. She is yours already. You cannot steal what already belongs to you. You hear me? She is yours. And here is your proof," replied Olga in one breath while wiggling Chrysa's letter in front of her brother's face.

"Maybe there is another way. Maybe I can talk to her baba, make him understand," Pauper said in a pretty unconvincing tone.

"There are no maybes in love. And you are a fool to believe that Master Calliga would come to his senses and hand you his princess just like that. This type doesn't know anything about love. For these people it's all about money and power. These people don't have souls. I am older and I know better. I've seen them in action. This was the type that sent me to America. You think I wanted to leave? Abandon my family and live like a peasant," Olga questioned with anger looking straight at her brother's eyes.

Olga was referring to something that Pauper had no idea about. Something that had happened many years ago when she was still a fifteen-year-old girl, something pretty dramatic, which had cost her virginity and later on became the reason that forced her to leave Greece. That something was an accident. Her first accident, the second and third were still to come. But for now let's focus on the first. So Olga's first accident occurred on an October afternoon, a few days before a Greek national holiday when Olga, excited and proud, stepped on a chair to practice the poem she was planning to recite in front of her classmates at the school celebration. Her mama and her baba were there, watching. When Olga finished the poem, they clapped happily. It was between clappings that Olga slipped off the chair and crashed on the floor. She managed to get zero external wounds, only an internal one which was deep and damaged her prospect to get married. The medical diagnosis was stiff and rigid. "The chair's leg tore your daughter's maidenhead. It's beyond repair. With a maidenhead like this I guarantee you no decent man would ever want her," the village's doctor said to Olga's mama. Kyra Vana, who was a pretty open-minded woman, disregarded his words, made up a nice white lie for her daughter who was anyway too young to realize what was going on and decided to bury the incident in her heart. But Kyra Vana's decision made no difference. Within days the medical opinion became public knowledge, something that made Olga's teenage years hell, something that later on forced her to grab the first opportunity to leave for good. Once she was in America the incident was erased from the villagers' memory, but Olga kept it between her heart, her legs, and her mind. Time and place transformed bad feelings and emotional wounds into a lifetime lesson. Beliefs, faiths, ideas even habits were built upon the experience of that accident. She started developing a repulsion, which later became a mega dislike for people in any high posts: officers, lawyers, doctors, landowners. She had a weakness for secretaries, nurses, workers and most of all victims of any type. She avoided clapping and denied sitting on wooden ordinary chairs; instead she preferred stools, love seats and old wide sofas, a habit that Betty Mulatto found extremely eerie and exceptionally bizarre. That was one side of Olga's personality, which she liked to call the feminist side. The other side was the side she was still developing after reading tons of romance paperbacks and trashy magazines, her sweet, sensitive, feminine side. So feminist and feminine were like covers of the same book. Which were the front and which the back depended on place, time and situation.

Thus Olga, after reading Chrysa's love letter No. Two and studying her brother's emotional condition, flipped from feminine to feminist and asked with a confident optimistic tone in her voice once again, "You think I wanted to leave? Abandon my family and live like a peasant?" Then came a brief pause, an opportunity for Pauper to nod or say something indicating an understanding. But Pauper didn't say or do anything, just stared at her. So Olga took a deep breath and went on.

"Listen to me brother, people would do anything to hold you back. If they sense that something is out of the ordinary they would cut your heart in half 'cause they are like wild animals; thirsty for blood, hungry for fresh flesh. And I am telling you I will not let them do even the tiniest scratch to you. I have learned the rules. This time I am ready to win the mega battle. This time I will show them what I am capable of."

Pauper stared at her with surprise. What a woman! He wondered silently and then, that's definitely an American woman.

Olga exhaled all the air out and continued, "Do you love her?"

Silence.

"Do you love her?" she repeated, once again focusing into her brother's eyes.

"Of course. Of course I do," said Pauper.

"That means you are ready to do the right thing. Right?"

"Right!?" mumbled Pauper between his teeth.

"That's my brother, that's my brother," repeated Olga a couple of times with great satisfaction and then, "I will help you. Just leave everything in my hands. Don't you worry. In less than a week you will have her in your arms." Then she pressed her body up against Pauper's chest, gazing at the mega sky and said, "For love's sake, only for love's sake."

The Emergency Meeting - Princess's Daughter

When Kyra Vana arrived at Madam Papadimou's, Kyra Soto, Puta's mama, was already there, trying to digest the mega news about Mrs. Calliga's missing tit plus Chrysa's upcoming wedding to the rich lawyer from the capital. So Kyra Vana entered unsuspected at first but as soon as she set eyes on Soto's face she realized that something was about to change her sluggish, loose, ouzo-type of mood. Note here that Kyra Vana disliked Puta's mama big time. And she had a good reason for disliking her. Kyra Soto was known as the mega storyteller, the greatest lie fabricator in the whole market while Kyra Vana was the frankest person in the entire solar system. If you were to ask Kyra Vana's opinion about Puta, you would have received a sympathetic gaze plus a heavy pitiful sigh for an answer. If you were to ask her about Puta's mama, you would have received the Greek version of the finger (the thumb between the index and middle fingers), a double spit (ftoo-ftoo) and a triple word blasphemy (Fucking Farty Faker). Keeping that in mind, neither Madam Papadimou nor Kyra Soto were expecting Kyra Vana to be in a cooperating mood. And they got what they expected: a bloody furious response, topped with extra layers of sour cream and mega bitter cherries.

"My son wants whose daughter?" Kyra Vana blared, spitting all over Kyra Soto's face.

"You know who I am talking about. Calliga's wife. We used to call her princess when she was still single 'cause of the way she wore her hair;

in a high tight ponytail with a golden ribbon framing her forehead," said Madam Papadimou while her lower lip vibrated like a piece of red Jell-O.

"Princess???" Kyra Vana repeated skeptically, avoiding eye contact.

"But we thought you knew about your son and princess's daughter," added Kyra Soto beseechingly.

Kyra Vana grinded her teeth, waved her hand at the two women as if to dismiss them, and looked the other way.

"Don't go away, we gotta do something about this, you are a mama and like any other mama you want your child's happiness," Madam Papadimou rushed almost in a single breath.

"What I want is to be left alone," replied Kyra Vana sharply while heading for the door.

"But princess's daughter is in love with your son too. Princess's daughter is..." started Kyra Soto once again, but she was forced to zip it up in no time.

"Shut up and listen to me, Soto. First of all, as far as I know this village has got no princesses. And second, if my boy is in love with Calliga's daughter it isn't my business. Is it? Is it ?" Kyra Vana yelled, grabbing Kyra Soto's long oily braid, still griddling her teeth.

"Nah, nah," murmured both women staring at her.

Kyra Vana sent them a long angry look, then exhaled vigorously on Soto's face, letting the braid slip out of her hand, and exited the scene.

For the next ten seconds the atmosphere crystallized. The two women made no moves. Their bodies froze along with their thoughts. Only their ears were in full operation, listening to Kyra Vana's heavy steps fading steadily and slowly.

When there was nothing to listen to but their own breaths, Madam Papadimou put together the last kilo of her courage and said, "What a woman! I knew she was tough but I didn't know that she was also hard-hearted."

"Bullheaded is the word," Kyra Soto added, straightening her braid with her clumsy fingers.

Kyra Vana might have been many things but she was neither hard-hearted nor bullheaded. At this specific situation she was just a betrayed woman. Yes, yes, yes. You read correctly. So I repeat once more: just a betrayed woman. And here comes the explanation, the short and efficient version. Several days ago and precisely the day that Kyra Vana's almost full-time-drunk-husband died Kyra Vana found in his pocket a letter. In that letter the drunkard was asking basically for two things: 1) forgiveness for his ouzo weakness, and 2) understanding for not devoting his heart to his marriage. Well, well, Kyra Vana thought looking at the letter, who was to think that the poor man realized that his drunkenness had deprived him from a devoting heart and a good marriage? The poor fellow wasn't as out of it as he had seemed after all. But when Kyra Vana turned the page over it was as if she had accidentally changed channels going from *Gone with the Wind* to *Rambo*. On the other side of the paper was the mega hangover you get after a night of infinite booze and great fun. No! No! No! It wasn't ouzo that forced Kyra Vana's husband to lead a pretty unfocused blurry kind of life. It was love. Love for another. The thirsty dehydrated type of love. The kind of love that needs witchcraft to get dissolved, but unfortunately Kyra Vana's husband didn't believe in witchcraft—only in the Greek Gods, and more specifically in Dionysus.

"Who is that damn slut you were trying to forget all those years, gulping all that ouzo while wasting my life?" asked Kyra Vana in full rage, while her eyes were skipping lines, looking for a name of the person in question. But the dead left no name, just a vague royal title, "The love for my princess," he wrote, "will die with me." Pretty melodramatic tone for a drunkard of his type. But who said that drunkenness lacks melodramas? No one I know off.

So Kyra Vana was left with an anonymous rage, which put her in black veils and extra silence. But anonymous rage is easy to forgive and becomes much easier when it involves a dead loser. And by the next day she had already decided to forgive her husband. "What the hell," she murmured, "he had his princess in his dizzy head while I had my Fragile in my arms. Not a bad deal." So she took a big drag from the flask of ouzo the deceased left her as the only memento and in no time her insides got on fire, her rage started to melt and a big smile sat heavily on her lips. Then she looked once more at the letter. "Well, well, my drunkard, you are dead and I am alive and God may bless the years ahead," she said tearing the letter into small pieces. Then she emptied the rest of the flask of ouzo into her mouth and decided to bury the story forever.

But forever proved to have a pretty short expiration date, and a few days later when Kyra Soto said that Pauper was in love with the princess's daughter, Kyra Vana put two and two together and came up with four, needless to say, she was pretty good at math. All of a sudden the anonymous rage was born, Kyra Vana's heartbeat got into high speeds and there she was grabbing Soto's braid and grinding her teeth furiously. Of course she didn't go on explaining the real reason for her behavior. Thus neither Kyra Soto nor Madam Papadimou came close to comprehending the real cause for her emotional outburst. But real comprehending requires good intention, something that Kyra Soto and Madam Papadimou lacked big time.

My Pretty B's

Besides their dual state of existence (two cheeks to a butt, two boobs to a chest), butt and boobs have a dozen other similarities. And this is a fact, not just my micro-personal opinion. Imagine: I am in mama's bedroom, in front of her mega mirror, naked almost as I was born if you subtract the white cotton socks plus the red scarf tight around my neck (note here that I am not copying one of Kundera's characters I am just trying to hide the hickey I woke up with), and I am eyeing my boobs and butt.

I am semi-circling, making half turns in order to get the visual going, and it's something like this: butt to boobs, boobs to butt, boobs to butt, butt to boobs. And I am thinking that if I were only to do this at the right speed I would be viewing my boobs on top of my butt or my butt underneath my boobs, placing both treasures in the same visual frame and rediscovering the moving image technique all over again. Anyway, since rediscoveries are beyond limits, I end up only with a piece at a time: butt-turning-boobs, boobs-turning-butt. After a couple of semi-turns I conclude that I have a pear-shape butt and upside-down butt-shape boobs, that's similarity No. One. Here is what I am talking about so you don't have to over twist your imagination.

So what do you say? Well let me tell you what I think. I think I am on the road to mega maturity. Do you know what I can get with those boobs and that butt? Almost any tsootsoo on the market. I was going to draw a tsootsoo sample map here but as you can see from previous sketch I lack Dali's artistic talent so please feel free to use your imagination. As I was saying, with this pretty pair of double b's (butt and boobs) I can get almost any tsootsoo on the market and that's a 100 percent guarantee—no fucking bullshit. So I stare and stare at my treasures and after a few minutes of staring Wicked Yiayia comes to my mind and for the first time I feel sorry for her knowing that her butt feels pretty unrelated to her boobs (or boob to be precise). She must be in a very imbalanced situation without that big boob of hers. I mean, just take a look at the following:

And since I am in this splendid creative mood I run, as I am, downstairs and share my thoughts plus sketches with mama who is preparing breakfast. Mama takes a good look at me from scarf to socks then releases a disapproving grimace and announces that my thinking is totally out of line. I am not sure which line she is referring to, but once again she reminds me that we don't function on similar mental frames and there is no way to broaden her horizons. I mean she cannot even sense that this is a truce gesticulation, another way of showing my willingness to hear her out, give her for the 100th time the opportunity to deliver the true version of the story and tell me who the fuck is my real baba. Anyway as I said mama doesn't get it but at least she doesn't get angry, so she pulls one edge of my scarf and says, "Come on beauty go and get some clothes on and come eat your breakfast. You'll be late."

So here I am, once again in front of the mirror, eyeing my front, my back and my sides, and I am thinking that if Mrs. Dimou had not come for her annual visit and Bo hadn't offered to tell me my family story I would have been swimming in deep dark waters, knowing nothing about my past and hoping too little for my future. I mean to learn if mama got married to baba like a mega whore. Lacking the only gift a missy of her time used to come with, her maidenhead, that's extra-large news to me that I grew up with a totally different version of the story. It's about a week now that I've discovered the old news and I finally feel okay with it. So what? She wasn't a virgin as she claimed to be. Anyway I am not so cool as I advertise. People do and say totally different things and it's totally okay as far as they only mess up the puzzle of their own fucking life. Right? Of course mama went beyond personal puzzles but today is the day to be forgiven. So I slip into my pair of jeans and a white t-shirt (going as a rebel, no bra no panties), and get downstairs for breakfast.

"For once wear a skirt. Here is your toast. It's almost eight," Mama says in sharp sentences, pouring coffee and circling around my head.

"Yiayia is coming for dinner tonight. You better change to a dress when you come back from school. I don't want to hear her complaining. And why are you wearing that scarf around your neck?"

For a minute I say nothing, just sensing the waters knowing that if I don't tell her right now I might run out of compassion. So I take a deep breath and, "I can go to the hospital for that blood test," I verbalize with compulsory coolness. But mama says nothing, just moves nervously behind my back reorganizing the dishes, which are already too organized.

"I agree to go to the hospital for the blood test you asked," I repeat slowly, smoothly.

"Well then, I'll try to make an appointment for this coming Saturday. You can go before visiting your baba," mama says finally, still behind my back, avoiding eye contact.

"So I can tell him whether his blood matches my own. Right?" I ask, but I hear no response, no moves, no reorganizations, no words, just a mega pause.

"Right?" I say louder, smirking inside but keeping it stiff and serious outside.

"Cough, cough," mama clears her throat letting me know that she heard me and then, "No! You can actually show him that you are HIS daughter. That's what you can do."

And as soon as she finishes her sentence, she bursts into loud tears. I don't see this but I hear it and although I lack the visuals I feel pretty uncool. *Fuck, and I thought the crying period was over*, I think, and I fill my mouth with too much toast, trying to survive the moment.

"Ugly things can happen to pretty people, you know? Just like that, without asking for permission, they jump on you and there you go, your whole prettiness is messed up. BLR. Beyond Local Repair. So what do you do then?" She asks mewling and wiping off rolling tears. I know that she expects no answer so I keep my jaw from moving and the answer arrives after a weepy pause, "You know what you do? You do what I did. You do what I did 'cause you love your life and you want to be pretty once again. Right? Right?" she asks, now determined to get a reply.

I nod, staring at the floor, swallowing the last piece of my toast, thinking that at soggy moments like this I feel like I am made out of sugar, dissolving in a cup of hot tea. And while I am stretching my sentimental walls, listening to my heart pumping an octave higher, my mind questions, is my real baba a *jumper* or a lover-slash-fucker? If I can get an answer to that, life will regain its initial state of prettiness. Only then the world will be able to grasp once and for all how *fuck off* came to be a disgusting insult and *jump off* its praising antidote.

Ancient Era

~~~~~~~~

Two Types of Truth

For Chrysa there were two types of truth: the single-vision and the multi-vision, and although she believed that fiction required telling neither of them, she knew that life promised both. And lately her life proved to be pretty right on the dot, keeping its promises to their maximum, stuffed with single-vision and multi-vision truths all at once. But before leaving fiction for life, let's elaborate a bit more about Chrysa's beliefs on truth. When Chrysa was young, fresh and still Calliga's favorite virgin, she thought that truth came in two types, two brands, two varieties, like the Fat and the Skinny.

The first type, the single-vision truth, had a monochrome clear-cut factual attitude, accepted no changes and lacked the evolutionary skills. It was stagnant and lived without an expiration day, simply forever like diamonds. The single-vision truth had nothing to do with maybes, perhapses, nowheres and somewheres and a lot to do with thens, nows, heres and theres. In other words, a single-vision truth stuck to a specific year, specific month, specific day, specific hour and pretty often to a specific minute and occurred within a specific planet, on a specific continent, in a specific country, village, neighborhood, etc, etc. A perfect example of a single-vision type of truth was the mega kiss on September 1, 1963 at 11:37 a.m., which occurred on Earth, in Europe, Greece, Artemis, behind GG's house, in GG's garden, near GG's sacred tree. Clearly that was a single-vision type of truth with all its chronological and geographical

94

specifics, the flat one-dimensional type, the type that allowed no hanky-panky.

On the other hand there was the multi-vision type of truth, which lived a multi-dimensional, multi-colored lifestyle, possessing a mega sensitive temper and an enormously adaptable attitude. A multi-vision truth was self-evident only to one's self and nobody else and didn't give a damn about time and place. By nature a multi-vision truth breathed on subjectivity and lived on personal opinion. For instance, a good example of a multi-vision type of truth was the great fortunate kiss-event as viewed by Chrysa, or the mega disgraced kiss-event as viewed by Mrs. Calliga, or the extra romantic kiss-event as viewed by Olga or the stupid kiss-event as viewed by Kyra Vana and so forth. So as you can see a multi-vision type of truth cares less about geography and chronology and more about people. In that perspective, a multi-vision type of truth possesses a sensitive heart, feeling for each and every person in life.

So now that we have the truth basics straight let's imagine Chrysa a day after the mega kiss, locked in her room, soaked in warm tears, and trapped between two types of truth: the single vision and the multi-vision. How does she feel? Totally confused. And in this blurry mood of total confusion, Chrysa touches with her trembling fingers her succulent lips, trying to think hard, hoping to clear up her mental fuzz and go on with her life once again. But life doesn't want to go on. Life is stubborn. Life has fulfilled its promises and expects Chrysa to fulfill hers. How? Well, well. An easy answer would be take two pills and call me in the morning but easy answers are hard to find and Chrysa knows it. So she takes a deep breath, wipes out her eye juices and decides to recap once more, focusing on the single-vision type of truth. Event, time, place. And the questions pop one after another in her mind. What happened? He kissed me. When did it happen? Yesterday. Where did it happen? At the church. Single-vision truth gets a mental checkmark and Chrysa exhales smoothly. And now she is ready to go on. So she asks, "Why did it happen? Was it fate? Fortune? Misfortune? Pure chance?" The last five questions have a pretty philosophical nature, requiring a lifetime to be thought, rethought and finally abandoned, so Chrysa ends up with a dozen extra kilos of confusion and a hundred kilos of energy. Thus, she starts racing in different, asymmetrical directions all over her room, trying to find a solution. Ten minutes later she gets tired and the image of Pauper comes into her mind. For a second the scene becomes static, heavy, pensive, critical like a mega climax moment in your favorite TV soap. When the climax melts, Chrysa swallows her tears, puts on a firm, serious look, opens her desk drawer, takes out a piece of paper and voilà five minutes later she comes up with her first love letter to our hero (go back and read it, if you want).

And now let's jump forward. Two days down the road. Chrysa is once again in the same room, still locked but totally dry (she hasn't shed a tear in the last two days). Now her mood is a bit clearer, semi-transparent, like a steamed mirror. She has received Pauper's reply and considers herself fortunate. Obviously the multi-vision type of truth has come to life and Chrysa has safely filed it in her mental drawers. So now she is 120 percent sure that she is on the road to great romance. Of course she realizes that she has to deal with mama and baba who think that Pauper is a pauper and they are getting ready to offer their daughter to an extra large gentleman with extra money, extra years and extra appetite. But Chrysa fears not. On her side there is love, fate, fortune, wisdom or simply Kyra Sophia, her mega supporter who has been the messenger of love, hiding the love letters between her boobs and advising Chrysa all the way. More specifically, at this very moment Kyra Sophia is standing over Chrysa's shoulder, dictating one word after another. And after four minutes and two seconds of serious thinking and slow dictation, Chrysa's love letter No. Two is ready. And it goes like this,

My dearest,

I am so sorry to hear about the death of your father. I cannot imagine the emotional pain you are in. Please keep in mind that I think of you every minute. Unfortunately, my parents fail to see the power of our love. They are forcing me to marry a gentleman from the capital. Of course I have denied their proposal repeatedly but they seem to ignore my wishes, arranging a house dinner within a day or two. I am not sure how I will be able to excuse myself. Anyway I don't want to trouble you more. I live only for your next reply.

Truly yours,
Chrysa.

PS: Remember I'd rather die than find myself in the arms of another.

And the reply comes the next day. So Chrysa reads while we peep over her shoulder.

My Chrysa,

I am sorry to hear that your parents aren't able to understand how strong my feelings are for you. I would have never thought to go against their wishes but I see no other option. And now I need you to look inside your heart and tell me, are you ready to follow me? Are you ready to do everything for your love? Our love? Are you ready to be mine forever?

If yes then we must act quickly, before it's too late. Let's become one forever and ever.

Yours.
Pauper.

Chrysa squeezes the letter against her chest and exhales deeply. A couple of seconds later she releases a huge toothless smile and falls into Kyra Sophia's arms, shedding the first tears of joy.

"I will be his forever, his and only his," she mumbles.

Obviously she has no idea what the future has in store. But then who does anyway?

A Bastard is a Bastard is a Bastard (Wednesday, September 25, 1963)

❝ Mama will be here any minute. There is no time for it. And I got my...my..."

"There is plenty of time. Get on," Master Calliga orders Maro as he pulls her little body and places it on top of the kitchen table. Once inside her, he starts pushing and pushing and pushing. Eyes closed, mouth half opened, face red like a beetroot, getting in & inner, inner & in.

Stop pushing so hard, Maro wants to say, but she is too occupied trying to make out the whereabouts of the second hand of the big clock that hangs in the middle of the kitchen wall. As far as she can see from where she is there is no second hand, only the big one, pointing straight at twelve, firm and fixed without plans to move anytime soon. *What the hell?* She thinks trying to stretch her neck a bit longer.

"Where is the second-hand?" she says.

"Who?" the Master utters while rubbing her tittie with his callus palm, still pushing with all his weight. Wasn't it like yesterday when he laid her for the first time on the kitchen table reaching for titties and found nothing?

"Ha! Your upper fruits need a bit more time but your lower is just right," he murmured at the time making his way between her thighs. Well, that was long ago. Today, four years later, Maro is a full size woman, with perfect tits and all, squeezed underneath him once again.

"The clock got no second hand. No second…" Maro goes but the Master draws his fingers over her lower lip and doesn't let her finish.

He doesn't like talking while doing it. He doesn't like talking in general. *You just keep your legs open*, he wants to say, but he swallows the words, thrusting it deep and deeper. Quick and quicker.

"It was underneath the big one. Stupid me. That's why I couldn't see it," Maro goes on, smiling.

"What?" the Master yells, saliva running of his mouth.

"The second-hand was underneath the big one," Maro says once again staring at the clock in full confusion.

"Shush! You can't put your tongue to rest for a second. Can't you?" he utters, pumping out the words in short breaths.

"It can't be twelve. Can it?" she asks and then, "Stop pushing. You are hurting me."

But he doesn't listen. He has almost reached the mega peak, giving out his last jostles.

"Ow! You are hurting me," Maro moans louder this time.

"Oooh!" He goes and is through.

"You can't shut up," he says, trying to catch his breath, still on top of her.

"It can't be twelve," Maro repeats, without paying any attention.

"What are you talking about girl? Of course it's not twelve. That clock is out of batteries. I've told your mama to take care of it but she doesn't listen. That's where you got it from right? You and your mama. Never listen," the Master says pulling himself off Maro.

"What the hell?" he yells, looking at his thing while grabbing Maro from her wrist.

"I tried to tell you I got my…my…" Maro murmurs with a giggle.

"Damn it. Your bloody stuff is all over me. You can't keep your mouth shut but when you ought to speak you…you…Well, what do you expect? You are only a bastard. Can't even keep your legs steady," the Master mutters, wiping the blood off his thing.

"You gotta go, mama is going to be here any minute," Maro smirks while pulling up her panties and a minute later she wears a sober, serious face and says, "I need to get a pair of new shoes."

"Money. Money. Money. You and your money," murmurs the Master and reaches for his wallet.

"And mama needs a new dress. A good one for Chrysa's wedding," Maro adds, looking at the paper bill that the Master is about to hand her.

"Ohh! It's never enough. Is it?" he murmurs pulling off another bill.

"That's it. I got no more," he says while he is patting Maro's rear.

"You know when I get married you'll have to spend a lot. Buy me the pretty dress, give a dowry and pay for the wedding party too." Maro smiles with confidence as she hides the money between her breasts.

"Who will have you? You are mine. You need no one else."

"Chrysa is Pauper's but the lawyer wants to marry her, so I can get someone from the capital too," Maro replies in a hurry, but as she looks at the Master's face she realizes that she has spoken without dipping her tongue into her brain so she covers her mouth and rushes away from him.

"Come here. What did you say? Chrysa and that pauper what?"

"Nothing, I said nothing."

"Son of a bitch. Who says such nonsense about my daughter? My daughter is my daughter and no one lays a hand on her. No one. You hear me?" the Master yells, grabbing Maro's wrist.

"What else have you heard?" he asks, waving a bill in front of her face.

"Well mama says that Pauper is gonna rescue Chrysa a day before the wedding. Sophia has the whole details but she pretends to know nothing," says Maro, smiling while keeping her eyes on the bill.

"That damned Sophia, I should have thrown her out of my house years ago," the Master murmurs as the bill slips off his fingers.

Rape or Love? (Thursday, September 26, 1963)

Three days before the arranged wedding...

"Do you love me or is your life miserable?"

If you knew him then, (I am talking about the old deluxe lawyer Chrysa's parents were about to grant their daughter to), you would have guessed by now that he was the only one capable of fabricating such a question. That was his type of question. The type that eliminates extra options, the type that presupposes your emotional state, the type that demands much more than a yes or no for an answer. The type that requires extra attention and smooth maneuvering. And if you were as young and fresh as Chrysa was, you would have smiled politely, lowered your gaze, hid your feverish cheeks between your palms, trying to survive the uncomfortable moment in full acid silence while planning your next move with mega charm and girly elegance.

Soon you would have realized that uncomfortable moments don't always drown in full silence. Some times they loll around forever becoming very uncomfortable, mega painful and finally intolerable, unbearable, simply excruciating. That's what happened three days before Chrysa's arranged wedding, when Master Calliga asked his daughter to keep her future husband company while he headed for the wine cellar to fetch a bottle of his best mavrodaphne.

But before going on, let's rewind and decorate the scene a bit more. It is a chilly autumnal afternoon, three days before the mega wedding and two days prior to Chrysa's rescue plan. A serene unusually peaceful atmosphere floods the Calliga Mansion. Mrs. Calliga is locked in her bedroom, lying in her bed; she had just gulped a handful of multi-colored pills. Her body is oozing with extra estrogen, her soul with mega hopes, her mind with glittering illusions, her upper lip with stiff new hair. Her wonder bra is hanging in the closet next to a long silvery velvet dress which was just made specifically for the big upcoming occasion. Kyra Sophia is at the butcher's, getting last minute orders. Georgia and Maro at the market, checking out their grocery list. Chrysa's sisters at Papadimou's atelier admiring their bridesmaid's dresses while their brother is at the church, delivering wedding chandeliers and ivory lacy ribbons. In that extra quiet house, at that pretty unusual hour for visits, (it's almost four in the afternoon), Master Calliga welcomes his future son-in-law with a cunning smile and anxious moves. But the welcomes don't last for long.

In fact the visitor doesn't even have time to sit down when Master Calliga calls his youngest and orders her to entertain her future husband while he rushes off to the basement. And without wasting any time the visitor pops the question.

"Do you love me or your life is miserable?"

Surprise! Surprise! Chrysa's eyes expand.

But the suitor doesn't wait for an answer. He walks towards Chrysa, then bends over and whispers into her ear, "'Cause I do. You are my only love."

Chrysa doesn't seem prepared for an erotic confession. Her heartbeat fastens, her mental flow clouds up.

"Do you love me or your life is miserable?" the suitor repeats looking into her eyes.

Why does he care if I love him? Chrysa wonders. *And if I say no? Would he understand?*

"Do you love me or your life is miserable?" She hears him once again. Now his voice is louder, exited, determined to get an answer.

My life is miserable all right, she thinks looking straight into his glittering eyes, which blink nervously. And for a moment Chrysa hallucinates. For a moment she imagines herself telling him the whole truth and nothing but the truth. For a moment she mistakes his hormonal excitement for a sympathetic anxiety caused by love. He might be able to understand, call the wedding off, she thinks secretly. But suddenly when she feels his breath on her face, she realizes that his intentions are far from sympathetic. So here we are imagining our heroine lowering her gaze, trying to survive the uncomfortable moment and failing big time. Mr. Future Husband is already too close to her, grabbing her from the waist questioning, "Do you love me or your life is miserable?" This time his voice is over-peppered, his breaths over-bumpy. Chrysa's face is in full blush; furious and angry she tries to think of the right answer. Of course she doesn't love him. Of course she hates him. But would an answer like that free her from this terrible moment? If a lie is capable of assuring her rescue, then she'll go for it. So she does.

"I do, I do love you," she blares trying to free her body off his hands.

"Oh my treasure, I knew it, I knew it," he whispers squeezing her tighter.

"Please, please keep your hands off me," she pleads.

"In a few days you'll be my wife," he articulates between heavy breaths, and shoves her on the sofa.

"I am not your wife yet," she screams, but now he is already on top of her. His mouth is all over her face, his hands in forbidden places. *Baba will save me*, Chrysa thinks. But baba is nowhere to be found.

"You are my treasure," he mumbles, tearing the flowery pattern off her dress.

"Stop it! Stop it!" she shouts, with tears filling up her eyes.

For Chrysa it's rape, rape, rape. Tears and blood fall in between. Simply a non-stop river.

"Rapist. Rapiiist. Rapiiisssttt!" she screams, stretching the word more and more.

"You are my treasure, my love, my wife," he mutters, his heart a blood pumper in high gear.

For him it's love, love, love. Hugs and kisses come one after the other. A passionate erotic game.

"My wife. My wifeee. My wiiifeee…." he sings as he forces her legs spread with both hands while he swings his body back and forth.

"You are a rapist! Rapist!" she shouts, once again with all her strength. But he can't really hear her. Now his erotic enthusiasm is over the edge.

"My treasure," he gasps, unable to control his moves, and then he collapses on top of her. The next couple of minutes he makes no moves. Holding on to her body, he tries to catch his breath. Time stretches. Heartbeats even out. And finally he manages to say, "You are my wife now," and pulls himself off her.

"You hurt me!" Chrysa whimpers in full shock when she sees the blood between her thighs.

"It will be okay my love," he smiles while his eyes try to meet hers.

"My God," Chrysa pulls her skirt off the floor and covers her thighs.

He makes an attempt to catch her once again but she is already in the other corner of the room.

"Rapist," she whispers with despair wiping the blood off her legs while he is zipping up his pants.

"My angel," he blows a goodbye kiss and exits the room.

The curtain falls while behind it Chrysa walks slowly, smoothly, as if the soles of her slippers don't touch the ground. Ten minutes later she is locked in the bathroom, soaking in warm water, her tears boiling with anger.

Street Violence

We are supposed to be at school. We are supposed to be practicing our bon-jours with Mademoiselle Papadimou, that's Madams Papadimou's oldest daughter. But instead we are at Bo's house. His mama is elsewhere for the next couple of hours. So here we are.

Our meeting is kind of emergency. The subject today is emotional support and surprisingly enough I am not the emotional supportee, but one of the supporters. Maria is the victim. The big news is that her folks are splitting up, gone to lawyers and everything, so Maria started splitting in. Internal demolition, Antonis calls it. A breakdown, Bo corrects him. A mega fuck-up, George argues. Whatever it is, it looks bad, ugly, dirty. It doesn't match Maria's high-class beauty. I say nothing for too long. I think too much for such a short period of time. The scene is unfamiliar to me and the rest of the guys except for Bo, who seems to be the mega expert on the matter, has witnessed too many divorces, has participated in infinite break ups.

Very nasty, nasty, civilized: These are the three types of separation. The three degrees of goodbye.

"In America three in five marriages end up in divorce," Bo announces with pride walking around the room with his hands in his pockets. He takes a long but shallow breath and goes on.

"My cousin's folks split half a year ago and now she lives like a queen, half the time in NY, half the time in LA. Her mama moved to LA with her new boyfriend. It's a pretty cool scenario. Her baba fucks a young chick half his age; he became a totally different man. So everybody is happy. That's why it's called a pretty civilized split. No hard feelings, no nothing. Of course you gotta have dough to end up like that. You gotta take care of the bills first and that's not always the case. My friend's folks had a pretty nasty one. Her old man caught his wife in bed with the superintendent of the building. He was also married. So they ended up having a double split. No one was satisfied, neither the fuckers nor the fucked ones. The fuckers stopped fucking and the fucked ended up with a lousy alimony and a lot of anger. And my friend not only has to work after school now but she also has to baby-sit her old man who is in a permanent shitty mood. That's a pretty nasty split, if you know what I mean," announces Bo, looking around for some type of reaction. But we are not reacting. His words are as if coming out of a TV set. So we sit tight and listen. And the show continues.

"Also my ex's parents split when she was only six. Her baba went for a business trip to California and never came back. She hasn't seen him since. That's also a nasty split but lacks extra details so it can't be characterized as a very nasty one. I mean there are so many examples. So many stories. I can go on and on and on. Splits are the new virus of our century. People split more often than they get together," Bo ends with a serious over-confident look on his face.

"That's impossible. You can't have more splits than marriages," George disagrees.

Personally, I know of no one who has had a proper divorce with a lawyer and all. In our village there are no divorces. Divorces happen only on TV, in the capital or in America.

"Yes, you can. You can split as much as you please. Split the split to its microform, to its atomic phase," Bo demurs and pulls his hands out of his pockets with a quick jolt.

At this moment Maria and Antonis exchange a tedious, lingering look. Although there isn't much light in the room Maria has been wearing her huge black sunglasses. They grant her extra style, as if she needs anymore. So she lowers the thick frame with two fingers (pointer and middle), the edge of her small nose barely holding the giant horn frame, then she takes a look at the top of the frame. A second later she pushes her glasses back and Maria regains her emotionless expression. All this time her long slim body is curled up next to Antonis, who has been chewing his pinkies with great concentration. I don't think there is much of them left. If he plans to avoid any bleeding, soon he will have to move on to the thumbs. Biting a thumb equals a big time fuck up. At least for Antonis. And a big time fuck-up equals a lot of thinking, which translates into extra large, mega silence and no looks of any type. And an extra large mega silence ends with a quick sucking of both thumbs, which leaves you with a bloody taste and a vampire's thirst. In that respect pinkies are lucky: they come first so they never end up bleeding. But as I said, it's early yet. At this very moment Antonis is still on the pinkies and although it seems that there is nothing left to nibble on, he looks pretty determined to make no moves.

"The thing is that Maria's mama isn't the tough type. You know, too sensitive, too touchy. So she complains about the usual abusive spanking," says George.

"That's domestic violence," Bo shouts with surprise as if he has just discovered something he had misplaced a long time ago.

"And domestic violence is a crime. A serious crime," he continues, yelling and staring at all of us as if we are the wrongdoers.

"How about street violence. Is street violence a crime too?" Maria questions stretching her legs lethargically.

"Cut the shit. I am not joking," Bo replies.

"Who says I am? Last time my baba performed his usual act it was in the middle of the street, in front of Loo's place. So, does that qualify for street violence? Tell us. What do they call that in America?" Maria asks, forcing a dry laugh.

Antonis stops the chewing and stares at Bo. And here comes the time we learn about a 24-hour help line for domestic violence. You call whenever you want. Day and night. And you don't even have to pay for the call. You call and someone is paying. You call and someone is there to listen. Day and night. Night and day. You give that someone your name and your address and the name of the wrongdoer and that someone notifies the police and the police come and arrest the bastard. It's a public service. Amazing stuff, eh? It sounds like the first part of a science fiction sequel. That's what I think anyway.

But Maria interrupts my mental excitement, "What if the police happens to be the bastard? Who comes to rescue you then?"

"Fuck. That's a pretty fucked up situation man," Bo says walking around the room now nervously as Antonis moves on to his left thumb. I pull out a Camel and lean back, getting ready for some enjoyment, but Bo cuts me off, "Can't smoke here. My old lady can't stand the aroma."

And then his face changes. Now he smiles, looking over-excited, almost happy.

What the fuck, I think but have no time to say anything.

"So it's great news then. I mean that your folks are splitting. It's good news. Your mama will be a free woman. The abusive bastard will get off her back for good. Right?" he asks Maria.

"Who said that a divorcee can have a better life?" Maria says and stands up.

Definitely not me, I think staring at Bo's frenetic look.

Ancient Era

A Dualistic Chaos (Friday, September 27, 1963)

When a person is declared an ass, he begins to act like an ass.
—Milan Kundera, *Immortality*

H ere we are two days before the arranged wedding. There is Chrysa once again in her bath. This time no tears, only bubbles, dazzling, glittering, gigantic bubbles with multifarious aromas and uplifting tempers. And our soggy Chrysa, questions in moist silence, *Why do I exist? What's my purpose in life? To whom do I belong?*

Pretty philosophical questions, right? Well, they seem so but they aren't, 'cause Chrysa knows nothing about philosophy; in fact, embarrassing to mention, but Chrysa doesn't even know her national fellow philosopher, Plato. Of course she has heard his name, but if you were to ask her who he was or when did he live you would have gotten a half-opened mouth and a dull look. Anyway, girls aren't supposed to have any bibliographical information stored in their beautiful heads but they are supposed to have beautiful heads and pure bodies. Our Chrysa has a beautiful head and forty-eight hours ago used to have a pure body too, but now, well...you know what she has now. And that bring us back to question No. One, why do I exist? She really means, in this miserable impure state of being what's the point of being alive? But what else can she do? She isn't the suicidal type and after all there is a place for whores in this world. 'Cause our heroine feels like a whore, a filthy little whore. And that bring us to question No. Two. *What's my purpose in life?* She is really asking, *what can a whore do?* A thousand things, if you ask me, but Chrysa knows nothing about whores; thus, she cannot imagine much. So she dips her head into the water, aiming to drown her shame but soon enough shame proves to be a good swimmer popping out brighter and glimmer than ever. And Chrysa's cheeks burn even more while her mind goes on to question No. Three. To whom do I belong? She squeezes her temples. Big thinking moments are on the way. And a few minutes later a howling murmur comes to life and it goes like this, "My heart belongs to Pauper but my body, my body?" And as Chrysa is falling for the same dualistic chaos that puzzled Descartes 400 years earlier, the door opens and there stands Kyra Sophia, Chrysa's guardian angel.

"Who are you talking to?" she asks with a smile while looking around. Her eyes are sparkling, her legs rush clumsily, her mouth is like a crescent moon swinging smoothly on its back. She comes close to Chrysa while unbuttoning the first few buttons of her blue cotton robe, bends over the bath and puff, her mega boobs release aiming for gigantic bubbles.

"It's your lucky day, girl. Here it is," says Kyra Sophia in a low voice and secretive tone. Her golden tooth shines proudly while she pulls a moist piece of paper off her hanging melons. "I bet this is it. Get ready to be in his arms in less than a day. Your worries are almost..." But before she has a chance to finish her sentence, she sees Chrysa bursting into tears.

"Oh girl. You tear my heart. What is it now? Are you sad 'cause you are leaving me?" Kyra Sophia asks trying to meet Chrysa's soggy eyes. "Don't you worry, it's not like you are going anywhere far. It's only a ten minute walk. I'll visit every day. Anyway you aren't supposed to cry now. You are only a few steps away from happiness."

But Chrysa's bursting, encouraged by Kyra Sophia's words, grows into a loud moaning. "I, I am not...he... he... the rapist...I am not ..." Chrysa says between squeezing eyelids and floating bubbles. All of a sudden Kyra Sophia's eyebrows are erect, eager to meet.

A cloud of skepticism covers her round face while gravity pulls her boobs with great eagerness. "Shush girl, shush. It's not time for tears now. Open the letter. Open it. That will make you feel better," she suggests, but Chrysa has no intentions of opening the envelope. She glances at the letter and her moaning becomes deeper, her tears thicker, her words more incomprehensible.

"What is it, my child?" asks Kyra Sophia enveloping Chrysa's face between her palms.

Chrysa takes a deep breath and starts talking slowly. Her eyes make an effort not to meet Kyra Sophia's. And a few minutes later Kyra Sophia knows the fucking facts—rape minus love plus blood and tears—and she is in total shock, spitting here and there, grinding her golden tooth and muttering "The filthy ass! The filthy ass! The damned filthy ass!" Is she referring to the lawyer or to the Master? Same difference, I would say. The sad thing is that her declaration is delayed, overdue, behind schedule. In other words she has declared an ass after the ass's shitty actions. So what good can that do? I would have guessed no good at all but Kyra Sophia surprises me. Kyra Sophia is not the type of woman who can be bossed around by my writing impulses so she spits her last mega mucus, buttons up her robe and says, "My poor child first of all let's see how we can patch up your hole and then let's stuff up their asses with their own fucking shit."

And of course Chrysa looks at her in total confusion. Patch up my hole? Stuff up their asses? Pretty inappropriate stuff for a missy of her type. So she says nothing, just stares at Kyra Sophia with juicy eyes.

"Come on girl, you still love him? No? You still want to marry him. Right?" Kyra Sophia asks.

But for an answer she gets a double sneeze so she opens the closet pulls out a big towel and as she hands it to Chrysa she adds, "You better get off that water."

"Wasn't me," Chrysa whispers stepping out of the bath with extra caution.

"What the hell?" murmurs Kyra Sophia. "Who the hell was it then?" she questions once again and starts walking around the room, her ears fully erect, her eyes totally expanded. She studies each corner, each crack, each closet but finds nothing. So she sighs heavily, then walks close to Chrysa and resumes her question in low volume.

"So you still want to marry him. Right?"

"Nod, nod and nod, nod," Chrysa's head goes.

"We gotta patch up your hole then. You aren't so fool to believe that he'll have you like that. Are you?"

"Of course not." Chrysa's lips finally manage to form a reply while her eyes wonder in despair.

"Now you are talking," Kyra Sophia says while rubbing Chrysa's body with the towel.

Current Era

Second-Hand Feelings Versus First-Hand Feelings

Once again at Loo's. It's Thursday afternoon. Cleaning day. Antonis is supposed to help Loo clean up his place and we promised to give him a hand. George, Bo, Antonis, Loo and myself all present. The only one missing is Maria.

"She is late as always," George complains as he passes the broom to Antonis.

"She is having a hard time, so give her a break," says Bo while wiping the tables.

"That poor girl is a mess," goes Loo, blinking too many times.

It's his eyes. His pupils are white. It's a bit freaky when you see him for the first time, but as you look and look you get used to it. In the end you find it cool, unique, mysterious. White pupils! Who would think of that? Nature. Only nature has such a bizarre imagination. So nature blessed Loo with white pupils, his folks with yellow ones and his oldest cousin ... well, his oldest cousin with no pupil, so he is pupil-less, at least in his right eye. His left one is normal; black and boring like ours. So who is the freakiest? George insists that they all are. In my opinion, they aren't freaky but ethereal, otherworldly. Loo's cousin, the single-pupilled, is charming. The absence of his pupil gives more space for the bright blue of his eye, which overflows making his right eye look bigger, broader, focusing nowhere and everywhere. It's the other eye, the normal one that seems limited, restricted.

"Maria is a thick-skinned girl, capable of getting herself out of any parental shit," goes George.

"But that's a lot, a lot of shit. It surmounts Mount Olympus," adds Antonis.

"It's also as ancient as Mount Olympus, so she is used to it. She has been sunk into it from the time I knew her," replies George, and I know that he wants to go on and compare Maria's situation to mine but at the end he decides not to.

"Did you tell her that we agreed to meet here at four?" I ask. Bo and George nod at once. Antonis just stares at me.

"Maybe she is helping her baba to groom the garden or something," I say and I know that I am being pretty unrealistic 'cause Maria's baba does nothing around the house except mess it up.

"Yeah, yeah, helping him beat up mama," says George.

"That man is too jealous," Loo says, and then he goes on to tell us a story about how Maria's baba almost beat a young fellow to death because he laid eyes on his wife.

"Was it only eyes? Nothing more?" asks George ironically.

"That's all I've heard," replies Loo without turning. Then he sighs and continues,

"And you know if he wasn't a policeman he would have been in jail by now. After the incident no one wanted him around so they found an excuse and relocated him. Maria was two years old when they arrived here. A precious little angel," adds Loo rolling his eyes.

"Each family has its own inside story," I say while scraping the window with both hands. There is a lot of dirt here to be cleaned up. Loo hasn't been taking proper care of this place. He can't. Anyway, there isn't a lot you can do with eyes like his. That's why Antonis has been helping him all these years. It's not really for money. It's more like charity work. He gets free drinks and we get a place of our own.

"I finished with the tables. What's next?" asks Bo.

"You can organize the drinks behind the bar," says Antonis, looking at Loo.

"Yeah, that's good. Do that," agrees Loo.

Loo talks like us. Coolly. George thinks that it's because he isn't married and has been hanging around alcohol too much. I think it's because of his eyes, his white pupils. That's the reason of his coolness. His white pupils let him see the world differently, freshly. Loo is the only grown up we can comprehend easily. He even talks in English. He doesn't have a huge English vocab but he knows the basics (all the f words plus their namesakes) and is eager to learn. *What's that and what's this?* he asks often, and then he listens. He concentrates, focusing his inner self into each word. He doesn't need to focus his eyes for you to know that he is listening. He doesn't need to look at you for you to know that he observes every move you make. Loo possesses internal eyes and those are better than the usual ordinary type. In Greek his vocab is monosyllabic, low, smooth. He doesn't make long sentences. He is a listener, a real bar owner, Antonis says. So Loo knows more than the priest and less than GG. And the good thing about Loo is that he is around a lot, not like GG who is impossible to find.

"Maria won't come," says Antonis, looking at the clock skeptically.

"Don't worry, she will. She might be collecting JAP's points. Or did she also decide to keep her legs sealed?" says George, looking at me.

"Just 'cause they stopped fucking you it doesn't mean that everybody else is in the same boat, you know," I say calmly.

"I am not talking about fucking I am talking about *jumping*, babe," George replies, looking around for justification. Antonis looks surprised. Bo seems indifferent. Loo sticks to his work as if he understands nothing. But I know he does. I know that our second hand English has more than second hand meaning for Loo.

"What do you know about *jumping* and fucking?" I ask George, looking straight into his eyes.

"Thanks to you I got a first hand fucking lesson," he replies angrily and immediately adds "lately it seems that fucking is your expertise."

"Fucking and *jumping*?" Loo wonders, "isn't *jumping* too Greek to be used as an English expression?" he asks scratching his head.

"At first I thought the same but once I started using it I started realizing that it started taking a different meaning, a meaning I wanted it to take so now I am convinced that once you start using a word in a specific way, the word revives itself and becomes a new word," explains Bo proudly in one breath. He looks around as if he is asking for permission to continue and then goes on.

"You see it's like English. When you all started conversing in English, you thought that you were conversing in a second-hand language. And when you converse in a second-hand language you feel less, words have less meaning to you. No?" And without waiting for a reply he continues.

"So at first a second-hand language gives you second-hand feelings and that keeps you at a safe distance from reality. You believe that you have authority over your heart. You believe that you alienate yourself from whatever good or bad happens around you just because you converse in a language you don't fully understand, or better said, you don't fully feel. It's like being an actor in your own life. You play your role but at the same time you are able to watch yourself, you watch your own life like it is someone else's life. Of course as time passes you get more and more comfortable in that role, you start forgetting how you started and once you forget that you are unable to look back and distinguish yourself as you used to do. So at this point you are still conversing in a second-hand language but you feel first-hand feelings, if I can say that. Right? And once you feel first hand feelings your second-hand language takes a different meaning. It simply becomes your first. At that point even if you speak in second-hand or in your premium your feelings have the same depth. Right? It's that simple!" Bo announces with enthusiasm, gazing thoroughly at each one of us.

Are we supposed to reply? Are we supposed to agree? Are we supposed to argue? I am not sure what is to be our role. So I look the other way and wait for someone else to take the initiative.

"So you are saying that emotional alienation needs more than a language switch. Right?" asks Antonis, gazing at all of us.

"I am saying that it doesn't take a long time for a word to grab a new meaning. It doesn't take a lot of time for a second-hand language to become a first-hand weapon," says Bo holding the same proud look.

"Definitely it takes less than we've anticipated," Antonis adds skeptically.

No other words are said. We keep cleaning immersed in our thoughts. Now and then Loo whispers a lingering tune and Antonis follows him but it doesn't last for long. I can't tell if it's in English or Greek. I can't distinguish the words. It sounds more like a melancholic mumbling. It's getting late and we all know by now that Maria won't make it.

From One F to Another

Who wears the balls in this house? Who wears the fucking balls in this house? You are fucking dead, totally fully entirely dead. So what can you do? Nothing! I am telling you, you can do nothing! Mega fucking NOTHING. You can't even enjoy your booze. The only thing you can do now is stare at the roots of the smartweed growing on top of your mega gravestone. Right? That's the only fucking thing you can do. So how does it look? Fun? How does your fucking princess look from there? I bet she looks tall, big and single-titted. Well let me tell you, your vision is good 'cause she just got promoted to the mega single-titted princess of the year. Damn well you heard me right, the mega single-titted princess of the year. Like a Cyclops, only the modern version— the two-eyes, one-tit type, that's your mega fucking princess. That's your..." Kyra Vana was cursing in front of the deceased's flask. Was she angry? Well, yes and no. One thing was certain: she was drunk, drunk and lonely.

No one was around. No sons, no daughter, no Fragile, no patchouli. Just her and the booze. Deep inside Kyra Vana wasn't angry with her almost-full-time-drunk dead husband or his single-titted princess, she was angry with herself. Angry that all those years she didn't assemble the guts to escape the boring scenario of her life and go elsewhere to start a new and fresh chapter. What was it that held her back? What was it that kept

114

her from living out her dreams? Was it fear? Fate? Faith? Or some other fucking f word she couldn't think off?

Questions like the above popped out like wild mushrooms in the deep forest. Questions that vacillated in her mind like the booze vacillated in her stomach. And how do you find answers to your own questions? Once again you go back to the f words. You FOCUS! Focus within. Focus within yourself and quit focusing elsewhere. So Kyra Vana closed her eyes and turned her attention within. She could detect a strong stink of ouzoness so she decided to move on and threw her head back with smoothness and headed for the next mega department. And as she stood there feeling her heart, a veil of sadness started steaming up inside her. Her bloody heart was pumping in mezzo forte but wasn't getting anywhere, and her veins were buried underneath deep dust, her arteries were blocked with boredom.

"What's wrong with you?" Kyra Vana asked. "Toock-toock," the heart tried to twiddle in waltz tempo but dust and boredom stood in the way. "What's the matter?" Kyra Vana attempted once again. But still she got no reply. So she placed her palms on top of her heart and tried to go beyond acoustic responses. For once in her life Kyra Vana was determined to get into the heart of her heart's problem. And where there is determination there is no dust or boredom.

"Tick-tack and toock-tick," the heart sent a cryptic message and Kyra Vana's face brightened up. Her fingernails tickled, she started feeling a weird excitement in the base of her stomach, her toes were on the alert, her emotional compass was spinning faster than ever. So she opened her eyes, stood up, pulled out the kitchen drawer and reached behind all the little zincky micro-pans. After a lot of reaching and a bit of zincking, she pulled out a big canvass bag and started filling it up with a few clothes, some food and a couple of herbs. When the bag was almost full, she took off her long black robe, hung it on the hanger behind the door and slipped into a bright red dress, then combed her long gray hair into a braid, put some patchouli on her cheeks, picked up the bag and the deceased's flask and slammed the door behind her.

It was only minutes later that she got lost in the mist of the night along with an unfamiliar tune. "Ta-ti-tok, ti-ta-tok, ta-ti-tak..." Was it her heartbeat? Was it her unsteady steps on the asphalt road? Or the shivering pine leaves? Well, no answers were given. So feel free to imagine whatever you like.

Lifetime, A Pretty Short Period

A day earlier, Olga put on her mega sombrero and started strolling through the alleys of Artemis. Narrow streets were filled with the aroma of basil, curious eyes peeped out half-opened windows, muddy kids exchanged marbles, ancient ladies dressed in black were dragging their curved bodies to the cemetery, cats and dogs were hanging off cracked pavements lethargically, sunburned old men rolled dice between their callused palms over a game of backgammon, petals of wild red poppies drifted through the breezy afternoon. These and more images. All there. All so close. All so distant.

Wasn't it like yesterday when Olga took the steamboat to America? Wasn't it like yesterday that her baba wished her a glamorous life with extra excitement and zero worries? Wasn't it like yesterday that her little brothers handed her a bunch of daisies and squeezed her tightly around the waist? Wasn't it like yesterday that her mama hugged her for the first and last time? Today and yesterday seemed so close and so far away. Now and then were like two sides of the same coin, and there was Olga standing on the rolling edge recalling the past and evaluating the present. What had changed? What had remained the same? Olga narrowed her eyes, tilted her head and started studying each corner, person and building with mega curiosity, trying to compare the saved images of yesterday with the real images of today, trying to recognize similarities, pinpoint dissimilarities, reincarnate the past through the present. But past wasn't in the mood for reincarnations, metempsychoses, revivals or any other resurrections for that matter. Past had passed and had no intentions of vicious repetitions. It was old, tired and bullheaded, wishing to be left alone in total peace and absolute serenity. And how does the childish and immature present look in the eyes of the old and wise past? Definitely, unquestionably, undeniably pretty unglamorous.

"Damn it, this looks small," Olga murmured staring at the main square. And then ten minutes later at the old pine trees outside the cemetery, "Those have shrunk, those have lost their pride." And in front of the city hall, "Can't be! What a gloom!" And with the same investigative look in front of Paradise, "too curved, too crooked." And last but not least in front of the Key-holder, her only teenage platonic love, "Pardon me, I didn't recognize you. You...you...grew up so much, you look like...like a mature man." She really meant, *What on earth happened to you?*

"And you! You! My Olga! You haven't changed a bit," replied the Key-holder while his pupilled-eye was running up and down in sprint mode. Olga took a few steps backwards, tilted her head even more, pulled off her big sombrero releasing her bleached mega hairdo and focused into his eye tensely. "You! You!" the Key-holder mumbled a couple more times deepening the tone of his voice, repositioning his pupil into the bright new vista. "You! You're pretty like a butterfly!" he finally managed to articulate. "With American long big wings," he added, smiling, and his good-eye glittered. Then he looked around as if he wanted to make sure that no one was listening and he asked in a rush, "It's the American air, isn't it?"

Olga said nothing, just smiled and lowered her gaze.

"I knew it! That's it! That rich air of yours keeps you fresh and bright," announced the Key-holder with mega thrill.

"Oh you are so kind, so so kind," Olga replied standing taller, fresher and brighter than ever. But the questions were:

Was he really so kind?
Or out of his mind?
Or maybe totally blind?

Well, kind plus a bit blind would be a rough estimate to the equation but out of mind, NO, he wasn't out of his mind. He might have been out of fucking, *jumping* and the rest for some time now but he was sane, sound, sensible and like most men of his type, full of shit. In other words, the Key-holder had noticed Olga's extra kilos, fresh wrinkles and fake blondness, but he was a gentleman and a good-hearted one. Thus he focused on the positives, and when you focus on the positives, you may not get a panoramic view but you definitely get a kaleidoscopic one. So he did. And as he was standing there puffing up Olga's exteriors, interiors started lighting up.

"You! You! You an angel from above. Me? Me just lucky to have a good eye to witness your beauty!" he exclaimed and click Olga's internal lights switched at once illuminating her perception channels and granting the unglamorous present with two kilos of style, five kilos of elegance and six kilos of charm which really sums ups to thirteen kilos of puffed-up ego. And thirteen kilos of puffed-up ego can get you a long way. OKAY maybe they cannot get YOU very far but they certainly got Olga out of her way. So instead of her planned destination 'cause she did have a planned destination, she ended up at Paradise. Of course at first she tried to refuse the Paradise-detour, but it seemed that fate was calling her. And who could refuse such an invitation? Definitely not Olga!

So it went like this: The Key-holder looked into Olga's eyes and asked, "You wouldn't deny me the honor to offer you a fresh drink, would you?"

Olga looked at her watch and nervously replied, "But I was going to the bank." And yes precisely right, she WAS going to the bank. She was going to the bank 'cause that very morning after a lot of thinking, calculating, and recalculating she ended up with an arithmetically generous decision: 100,000 drachmas. One hundred thousand drachmas (approximately 1250 dollars (1250 x 80)) was going to be the amount that Olga had decided to give to her brother in order to start his new married life with Chrysa. And one hundred thousand drachmas were precisely half of Olga's savings. In other words Olga had decided to offer half of her life's savings to her brother 'cause she believed in love and was determined to see it flourish. Obviously her brother knew nothing about it. It was Olga's mega surprise. She was planning to give it to him the day after Chrysa's rescue. She was planning to surprise them both. Vastly, massively, enormously. Of course much later Olga's plan proved to be a triple-surprise-plan, surprising not only bride and groom but mostly and hugely her own self. But that was much later. For now Olga was still standing nervously in front of the Key-holder who was trying to convince her to accept his invitation.

"It's only four, you have plenty of time to go to the bank. Plenty plenty of time," repeated the Key-holder. He sent her a meaningful look.

Olga jerked her head a couple of times, took three breaths of fire as she got ready for the next big event and started walking behind the Key-holder. The road to Paradise was short but filled with joy. And the destination? The destination simply paradisal. As soon as they got inside the Key-holder offered Olga a chair and a glass of lemonade. Olga rejected the chair politely, picked up the lemonade and headed for the bar. She chose one of the stools with care, sat on it and started swallowing small sips from her lemonade while looking around discreetly but obviously enough for the Key-holder to notice.

"So how do you find us? Old? Aged? Cracked by time?" questioned the Key-holder and his theatrical mood suddenly dropped like an egg on a frying pan.

"No! No at all! I mean things might look different to me. Things might seem…as…as…as different," added Olga at last, pretty disappointed with herself that she wasn't able to come up with a better word. And then apologetically, "It's also my Greek. You know what they say; if you don't use it, you lose it. So you better forgive me if my tongue is a bit stiff. But isn't it so nice to see everybody?" she said in a cheerful, happy tone.

"It isn't just nice. It's great! Great!" agreed the Key-holder dragging his erotic gaze across Olga's face.

A flirtatious breeze started filling up Paradise; gazes in lingering hypnotic modes, moves like alluring mesmerizing gears, heartbeats in full fortissimo. *What a blessing!* What a blessing! thought the Key-holder while leaning over Olga's cleavage. All those years he had developed a particular taste for deep moist cleavages, melon-shape bottoms and dried taut pussy-holes. All those years he had done nothing but stuffing up holes, squeezing smelly boobs and pinching rear-cheeks in various brothels. Quick, fast, clumsy personal moments executed in impersonal places. All those years his life was a sum of small-rush instants without significance, without memorable anamneses, without nostalgic feelings. But now? Now it seemed like time had stopped. Seconds got stretched. Thoughts got out of the way while heartbeats were announcing the beginning of a new era.

"What a blessing!" the Key-holder verbalized as if he was reciting the first rhyme of the most popular erotic poem.

"Cough! Cough!" Olga responded letting herself loose in the spark of the moment. "A blessing is to see you," she said, and as if she realized that she'd said something she wasn't supposed to, she immediately added, "I mean to see everybody, it's a blessing, definitely a blessing. A blessing from…frommm…"

"From above," filled in the Key-holder in a gasp gazing at the cracked ceiling as if Divine apocalypse was in its way. With a quick jump Olga rearranged her rear on the stool and followed his gaze. And above they were looking when out of the blue long cracks popped up from below. "Crack, craackk" and "craaackkk!"

Suddenly the stool's leg broke in four pieces and Olga found herself on the dirty floor of Paradise, with one leg pointing to the north and the other to the south.

"Ohh my my my…" mumbled the Key-holder in great awe and mega embarrassment. Quickly he bent on top of Olga, but when he focused carefully he realized that Olga was gone, off, lying there as if dead.

"Olga? My Olga," he called a couple of times, slapping her rosy cheeks.

Luckily enough Olga was far from dead, she was just shocked, dazed, simply traumatized. A second accident had occurred and although this one didn't seem as dramatic as the first, harsh feelings and bad memories started waking up. So for a couple of minutes Olga stayed still, frozen, crystallized, fighting internally with old monsters. Once the fight was over she exhaled, then slowly opened her eyes, focused on the Key-holder's pupil and asked, "How long does it take for a broken part to heal?"

"What broken part?" the Key-holder questioned anxiously.

"That one, at the end of the spine," added Olga while reaching with one hand underneath her back.

"The tailbone," replied the Key-holder skeptically and immediately, "the tailbone needs a lifetime to heal, a lifetime."

"Is that long?!"

"A lifetime can be a pretty short period of time," replied the Key-holder squeezing Olga's hand in his. And then he added slyly in a lower mysterious tone, "It only depends with whom you share it."

Olga blinked nervously, smiled shyly while wondering, *This can't be an accident. Can it? Can it?*

Of course it can dear, I would have said but hesitated. So I let her enjoy her last piece of happiness; after all she is our Feminine Feminist Fan and, as known by now, I possess a weakness for f fans of any type.

The Ritual Act

There was a rumor that Asian women had it the other way, the way lips rest on the edges of the mouth, while the rest of the female brand (non-yellowish) had it vertically like a buttonhole. Okay, okay. I admit it; I've confused you big time. But let me try to fill in the blanks. So once again. There was a rumor (note here that the past tense is used intentionally since the rumor isn't applicable anymore, maybe 'cause of its falseness, maybe 'cause globalization has managed to flatten out variations) that Asian women had it ("had" equals "possessed" and "it" equals "the female organ") the other way (meaning differently from the rest of the female population). And now the question is how the rest of the female population had it? I would have answered, in the normal way, but that would have been even more confusing so I leave the words for a while and pick up a pencil pleading for old pal Dali's help. And here it is

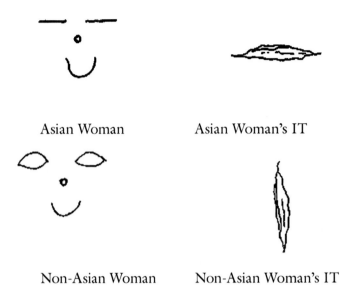

Asian Woman   Asian Woman's IT

Non-Asian Woman   Non-Asian Woman's IT

Okay I know Dali has lost patience and I've lost hopes of becoming the next mega painter of my time but I thought we had settled that in previous pages. Anyway I am going to remind you once and for all that you should disregard my artistic maiming and focus on the essence of the matter. Now do you get it? Good! So I am off to the next question: where did the rumor come from? The truth is that I have no idea and Pauper was in similar levels of ignorance but unlike me he knew one thing: that every man of his division before getting married had to check out the validity of that rumor. It was a ritual act. The bachelors' party of his time. So when his sister assured him that Chrysa was to be his wife in less than a week, he got pretty nervous. Basically two things caused his nervousness: 1) he needed money to get the ritual over with and 2) he needed more money to make the wedding a reality. So his problem was currency or, better-said, lack of currency. But who wouldn't sympathize with currency problems? Even Onassis would have. And as for Pauper's buddies? Well they were nowhere near Onassis so their sympathy was blacker than the black sea, higher than Everest and rounder than the full moon. Thus as supreme and loyal mates they knew what they ought to do and did it in no time, coming up with 468 drachmas, which was more than enough for the whole operation (the ticket to and from the city, the ritual act, plus a round of ouzo shots at Paradise where Pauper was to share the details of his ritual experience).

So here we are at Paradise, twenty-four hours before Chrysa's arranged wedding with the lawyer, four hours before the mega rescue plan, two hours after the ritual act and only a few minutes before the first round of ouzo shots. At that pretty intense moment Pauper looks at Dimitris's eyes, wipes his saliva off his mouth and starts the blah blah.

"Imagine an over dry prune, but not that dark purple color that common prunes come in. But a prune colored like a peach, an old decayed wrinkled peachy prune. That, that was what it looked like. I am telling you it was nothing like the widow's, which is juicy, and tastes like cherries and nothing like the gypsies', which is spicy and has the color of cinnamon. This one was sour, peachy and tasted like goat milk," Pauper said and exhaled heavily.

"You are saying that 280 drachmas went wasted on a decayed pussy that looked like a rotten fruit?" Fucking Auntie Puta asked Pauper with a mega disappointment in his eyes.

"Can't be right, man. Can't be right," hissed Loo, rolling his eyes and grabbing the bottle of ouzo.

"But how was it? The shape, was it different? Its lips? Its depth?" Dimitris went on as if he hadn't heard any of Pauper's words.

"I am telling you it was like a peachy prune. Nothing less, nothing more," Pauper stated seriously without making eye contact.

"And the shape?" Dimitris insisted louder.

"Like a prune. As far as I know prunes come only in one shape and it was exactly that fucking shape. What else can I say? I can't fabricate more than that," squeaked Pauper with a staccato tone.

"Fuck, man, that sucks," murmured Loo, looking at his cousin who had been in a weird over-silent mood all this time.

"So all that stuff they say about Asian pussies is just a mega fucking lie then, a mega fucking lie, eh?" muttered Fucking Auntie Puta swinging his head with disappointment.

"I can't talk about all the Asian pussies. I can only say that the one I had wasn't anything out of the ordinary, at least shape-wise. Now width-wise it was a bit loose but that might be 'cause it was overused. And lengthwise it was a bit short but that again might be 'cause I have it long," smiled Pauper, gazing proudly at the rest of the boys.

"Stop it man, we asked for a pussy description, not for your... your tsootsoo's dimensions," squeaked one of the boys at the other end of the room.

"Why not. A long detailed description of your mega king would do for me," yelled Fucking Auntie Puta and everybody burst into laugher.

"Come on, guys, let's drink to the mega operation. Tonight is the night. Tonight our friend will get his chick in his hands and live happily ever after. So let's drink to tonight's mega operation," the Key-holder finally said as he filled up the little shot glasses with ouzo. Then he took the first ouzo shot and handed it to Pauper and said, "Come on man, do us the honor."

"I am... I am not ..." Pauper mumbled a couple of times looking at the boys with hesitation.

"Shut up man and drink up!" ordered Dimitris authoritatively who knew Pauper's dislike for alcohol.

"A shot of ouzo will not make you a drunkard," added Loo, patting Pauper's back with a big smile.

At once all the boys gathered around Pauper raising the little glasses into the air and with big smiles and mega contentment started shouting, "to tonight, to tonight, to tooo..."

But the shouts didn't reach peak point. They were cut off as soon as they began with a long loud slam of the door, which sounded like "slaaaaammmmmm!!!" In no time all heads turned around. Pauper's young brother was standing in front of everybody, briefcase-less (if that's possible to imagine) with an out-of-place look, simply because he was out of place; Paradise wasn't his local stop. Of course he didn't look lost, just misplaced like a fly in a bowl of milk. *Something happened*, Pauper and Dimitris thought and exchanged a couple of nervous looks. At the same time the Key-holder and Fucking Auntie Puta looked around with confusion. A mega minute of wondering, speculating and guessing, led nowhere. Then Loo finally broke the crystallized atmosphere by asking, "Where is your briefcase man? You got robbed or something?" And bull's eye he hit. Pauper's young brother, the Aromatist as commonly known, took a few hasty steps and after a couple of puffs he explained that *some bloody, dirty gypsy* (to use his exact words) broke into his house, put a spell on his sister Olga and left with all his herbs.

"Yes, yes all my herbs," he insisted, staring at everybody with his big blue eyes.

Mister Aromatist had no evidence whatsoever about what he was saying. Yes, someone had gone into his house and took a small bag of lavender off his wooden cabinet but that someone wasn't a bloody, dirty gypsy and of course that someone didn't put a spell on Olga. The thing was that Mister Aromatist was a racist. He hated gypsies, floral scarves and watermelons. Gypsies 'cause they had a lot of dirt, no houses and too many kids, floral scarves 'cause they were worn mainly by gypsy women and watermelons 'cause they were sold mostly by gypsy men who merely stole them from the local farmers. So when Mister Aromatist returned home from one of his usual two-day trips and saw his sister walking around the room with a floral scarf on her head and a plastic bag of ice on her butt he panicked and started asking questions. Olga, who had just came out of a long heavy nap, wanted to be left alone so she answered none of his questions, just pointed him into his wooden cabinet which was in the middle of the room with all its drawers open.

When Mister Aromatist saw his cabinet in such a state, he lost his temper and started yelling while counting one by one all the herbs. Five minutes later when he finished counting he hid his cabinet and his suitcase under the divan, grabbed Olga's arm and demanded to know who was responsible for such a mess. Olga, surprised to see her little brother acting like a maniac, burst into a gentle witty laugh and, gulping a handful of painkillers, answered, "Agape, the only one responsible for this whole situation is agape. Who else can be capable of such a mess anyway?" So Agape it was, thought the Aromatist and headed for Paradise. On his short way there he put two and two together and came up with more than four. Minutes later when the story got out of his mouth with extra enthusiasm and mega certainty the Paradise boys had no other choice but to believe it. The only one who demanded extra info, specifically a full detailed description of Agape and Olga's condition, was the Key-holder, but when the Aromatist informed him that Agape is a filthy gypsy thief and Olga her only victim, he stopped asking and started smiling while gulping ouzo shots one after the other. It was at that precise point that the counting started. And it went like this:

Ouzo shot No. One,
        Ouzo shot No. Two,
                Ouzo shot No. Three,
                        Ouzo shot No. Four
                          and...

Current Era

Evolution's Fault

We cannot understand all the traits we have inherited.
Sometimes we can be strangers to ourselves.
—V.S. Naipaul, *A Way In the World*

I t's Saturday morning. I am at the clinic. Fifteen minutes earlier than my appointment. I am here alone without maternal support. Free and unembarrassed. I managed to slip off mama's detector while she was chit-chatting with Wicked Yiayia. So here I am in the lounge, trying to look cool, chill, frosty if possible. I nibble some fingers, I scratch off a couple of pimples, I twist a strand of hair. I admit giving blood isn't my thing. Blood, in general, isn't my favorite beverage. As long as I can remember most bloody experiences were far from thrilling. As far as I can recall warm blood doesn't shock me. And red isn't my favorite color either. It's weird to be made of something that you can't stand. But it's weirder to be made by someone you don't even know. Weirdness comes in many sizes and blood in many shades, I think, trying to lighten my mood and wipe away some of my fears. *Mega sissy, mega sissy,* Maria would have said if she was around like that day about two years ago when she forced me to push hard and harder. She yelled louder and louder. She got bloody and bloodier losing her virginity on our bathroom

125

floor over a bent tampon. Maria, my coolest friend, whom I haven't seen for the last several days now, seems to be afraid of nothing, seems to be made of the best brand of blood and the highest quality of flesh. Maria who rides life with attitude and calls me sissy on any given occasion. I think of blood and Maria comes into my mind, lying on our cold bathroom floor, her long ivory legs spread, biting her lower lip and making fists, ordering me to push and push and push. And me nervous, afraid, naïve, ignorant.

"Stop being such a sissy and do it," Maria ordered me that day.

So I squeezed my eyes while touching with my trembling fingers the edge of the tampon.

"Do it. Do it," Maria shouted spreading her legs wider.

Making an effort to push the tampon deeper, I gritted my teeth vigorously.

"More, more" and "more," she yelled. And less, less and less I pushed.

"Are you gonna do it or not?" finally she asked with anger.

"I am doing it," I protested.

"Well you aren't doing it right then," she complained.

"What do you want? I am not an expert. It's not my every day thing if you know what I mean," I objected trying to sound cool.

"We owe it to the liberation of our female generation. We, the females of the future, ought to be clean, clean of the evolutionary fault," Maria said and I stared in confusion.

"What evolutionary fault?" I asked, my two fingers still pushing between her vaginal lips.

"The next female generation won't be born with hymens and maidenheads. The next female generation will be physically equal with the male generation. It's evolution that didn't catch up yet so we are still born with that unnecessary fucking maidenhead. It's evolution that…" she went on while I listened perplexed, puzzled but happily curious. Wasn't it a great relief to hear that there was another way out? Wasn't it great news to learn that a young girl like myself could become as cool and brave as all those boys who hung around the school toilets comparing their tsootsoos and shooting off their piss? Wasn't it great that physical equality would grant me the ticket to the men's world? Of course it was. But the greatest news of all was that I could get my ticket to the boys' world without having to depend on them, without having to go through the P in V act,

(Penis in Vagina). The only thing I would need would be the stiff edge of a tampon, two friendly long fingers and a strong push.

So I pushed hard. I pushed with all my strength. I pushed without looking. And as I was pushing I felt Maria's fingers on top of my own. I heard her voice trembling. I saw her cheeks blush. I sensed the warmth. First there were just a couple of bloody spots on the yellowish tiled floor. Minutes later there was a ruby stream. Physical equality was restored and Maria was free to go.

"You know it's not so bad as it looks," she said minutes later as she looked at my frightened face. In reality I was more skeptical than frightened.

"But isn't it like we are forcing equality?" I finally asked.

"Perhaps, if you wanna see it that way," she replied with indifference.

"Well then forced equality isn't real equality," I stated looking straight into her eyes.

"Who says so?" she protested, smiling, and without waiting for an answer she added, "You are just a mega sissy. Nothing else, just a mega sissy." Then she came closer and enveloped my body with her long arms, kissing my face as if I were the one who was losing all that blood.

"My sissy," she mumbled, "my mega sissy. Let's get you cleaned up too. Let's wipe off evolution's fault from your body once and for all. Let's restore physical equality right now, right here."

"Here. Here!" The nurse's voice brings me back to the cold clinic. A couple of old ladies in black stare at me, questioning with their eyes who's I am and what I am doing here. I jerk my hair off my face and stand up. The nurse stretches one hand towards my side with a friendly smile while with her gaze appoints me to the room next door. I walk in front of her with steady steps; the sound of my heels echo through the long empty hall.

"Just sit tight for a sec," the nurse says and closes the door behind me.

In less than a sec the mega nurse arrives with a huge needle and a big smile.

"Can I see your left arm?" she asks without any introductions.

I nod and stretch my arm.

"The left one," she repeats and I smile apologetically. *Left, right,* I think silently pulling one arm in, the other out.

"That's right. This is your left, the arm of your heart." She smiles, showing some teeth while getting ready to thrust the needle into my skin.

"Look the other way," she orders me. I do as I am told. I feel a pinch and then nothing.

"You are all set. Free to go," she says, pressing a green band-aid with her thumb.

"When should I come for the results?" I ask.

"I'll give you a call in a couple of days," she replies sending me a don't-you-worry-look.

A few minutes later I am out, pulling off the band-aid from my arm, heading home.

"Mega sissy needs no band-aids," I say to myself and sigh with relief.

From Bloody Mary
to Bloody Chrysa & Vice Versa
The Evening Before the Mega Rescue

How can you transform a Virgin Mary into a Bloody Mary?

Well that's an easy one. Add some booze and you are ready to go. But the tricky question is: How do you transform a Bloody Mary into a Virgin Mary? Or coming back to our story, How do you transform a Bloody Chrysa into a Virgin Chrysa? Is it possible?

Well, well many bartenders might have been pretty perplexed with this one but Kyra Sophia had the answer and it was simple, pure and bloodier than ever: tomato juice. Of course Kyra Sophia arrived at that solution not because she was a simpleminded maid with a lot of bartending experience and no sexual expertise but because she was hugely fond of alternative, complementary therapies, believing that any medical or surgical approaches are either for those who fail to see the healing powers of nature or for those who lack the patience to look around.

So based on those beliefs she directed her willpower to the grand abilities of nature and came up with a pretty good plan. The plan would go like this: The first night of Chrysa's and Pauper's erotic chit-chat Chrysa was to hide a little plastic bag of tomato sauce underneath her pillow. Immediately after the P-in-V act (Penis in Vagina) and while Pauper would try to catch his breath, Chrysa would reach under her pillow, grab

129

the plastic bag and empty the magic pulp between her thighs. And voila! There would lay the physical evidence of her purity, the greatest gift a wife is capable of granting her husband, virginity à la tomato sauce with a half spoon of lavender and a touch of ground mint.

Needless to say, the latest ingredients would serve as sleek aromatic camouflages. Of course there was a tiny problem, the only aromatic/herbal provider in the whole area of northern Greece was Pauper's young brother, the Aromatist as known by everybody or periphrastically *the guy with the red briefcase glued to his left hand.* So if Kyra Sophia wanted to obtain all the ingredients for her sacred recipe she would have to go to the only provider.

In other words Kyra Sophia was faced with a similar problem that Mrs. Calliga had to face about fifty pages earlier when she was in desperate need of Puta's multicolored pills.

And how did Mrs. Calliga overcome her problem back then? By asking. After several sleepless nights and a lot of twisting and rolling around she finally realized that she had no other choice but to ask for Madam Papadimou's help. And because Mrs. Calliga was a full-class woman with a full-class status and a half class chest, she stretched her torso—single tit faced up—and employed her full-class influence on Madam Papadimou making her swear in front of GG's mega icon to mention her name to no one. When Madam Papadimou finished informing all the no ones she knew, Mrs. Calliga ended up with a plastic bag filled with Puta's colorful pills, a cheerful mood and a lot of gossiping behind her back. It was then that Kyra Sophia heard Georgia and her daughter, Maro, talking about her Missus, her tit and Puta's magical pills. It was then that Kyra Sophia thought that gossiping is like garbage; it stinks anywhere you leave it. Gossiping is naughty, bad, and totally unnecessary. Gossiping leads to nowhere. Of course at the time Kyra Sophia failed to see the informative values of gossiping. In other words she failed to recognize that sometimes gossiping could lead to learning, and learning to knowledge, knowledge to education and education to wisdom. Days later when she was faced with a similar problem she chose, thanks to gossiping, to ask no one for help, not even the Aromatist. So she put on her shoes, her floral scarf and her extra observing eye, sneaked into the Aromatist's house, and got what she needed. Surely her accomplishment wasn't so large as she thought it to be but it certainly looked bigger than normal. It happened like this:

When Kyra Sophia entered the single-room house, 100 percent convinced that no one was inside, she ended up face to butt with Olga. It was only a day earlier that Olga had smashed her tailbone on Paradise's stained floor, thus spending her latest hours totally drugged, face-cheeks facing down, rear-cheeks facing up. So Olga's weird position forced Kyra Sophia to freeze physically, mentally and momentarily. But as soon as the frozen moment entered its defrosting cycle Kyra Sophia started questioning silently, *what the heck is she doing in that position?* and *Is she out of her mind?* Of course it might have been the proper time for such questions but not for such answers so Kyra Sophia decided to go on and take her chances. Slowly she walked around Olga while her mind was racing, trying to come up with a good explanation for entering the house without knocking. But once again Kyra Sophia was faced with the unexpected: Olga dozing in some kind of day-dreaming; eyes half-open, lips hanging heavily, gaze focusing beyond the real world. So Kyra Sophia, without much thinking, took off her scarf, threw it on Olga's head and went on to examine the whole room with her investigative eye. Without difficulty she spotted the Aromatist's herbal reserves, which were tightly arranged in a wooden cabinet next to the main divan. Two minutes later she exited the house with a wide smile plus a handful of lavender minus her floral scarf. So mission-lavender was accomplished. Mint she had. Thus the only ingredient missing were tomatoes. Juicy, red, fresh tomatoes. So she headed straight for the Mansion and most specifically the Mansion's kitchen. Once she was there she opened the refrigerator and as soon as she eyed three big, succulent tomatoes, a squeaky voice pierced her head and made her heart jump wildly.

"Get away from those. Those are for Master's tomato soup," the voice ordered.

"What the hell are you doing here so late?" Kyra Sophia asked Maro and without waiting for an answer she bent on top of the refrigerator door.

"You cannot have those," Maro said, raising her voice even more.

Kyra Sophia turned around, sent a get-out-of-my-way look to Maro and once again bent over. But Maro wasn't about to give up.

"Those are for my Master's soup. You cannot have them. Are you deaf or stupid?" she yelled and placed her butt between the refrigerator and Kyra Sophia's angry face.

"WERE for his soup. WERE!" replied Kyra Sophia stretching her hand.

"Over my dead body," yelled Maro grabbing Kyra Sophia's hand and a sec later, "Come on show me your big muscles stupid old maid," she screamed pressing her lean waist against Kyra Sophia's ancient belly.

Kyra Sophia inhaled slowly, then focused her sharp gaze on Maro's face and said "I know where you got the money for your new shoes."

Maro smiled showing off her big shiny teeth and replied without hesitation, "And I know why you want to steal my tomatoes."

"So we are even. Aren't we?" asked Kyra Sophia without blinking.

For a couple of minutes Maro stayed still, saying nothing, as if she was solving some important mega equation in her head. When she finished, she took a step back, gazed at Kyra Sophia with satisfaction and said, "Even, we are."

A Sister Gotta Do What A Sister Gotta Do

Fighting her genes wasn't something Chrysa was accustomed to doing. How many times did she stand in front of her full-length mirror sucking in her belly or getting into an over-tied corset? Not many. Unlike her oldest sister Zoë, Chrysa wasn't following fashion tips. Simply because she had no need to do so. Her beauty was natural, required no molding, needed no airbrushing. A bit of waxing (an over fuzzy upper lip was all the unwanted she got stuck with) and she would climb up beauty pageants in no time. She was the Penelope Cruz type, only longer, curvier. And curvier was the winning brand at the time. In the early 1960s the sex appeal was curvy, (even coca cola possessed a lingering glass curved body) and curvy was Chrysa. Curvy hips, curvy boobs, curvy cheeks, even a curvy family name. So overall package? BQ in BQ (Best Quality in Best Quantity). P in P (Perfection in its Premium). A daughter you would be happy to have. A daughter easy to get rid of. That was Chrysa, golden and precious in her glorious years of perfection. Of course, like anything else, perfection comes with an expiration date and Chrysa's arrived with Pauper. After the mega kiss rumors were all over Artemis. They started as a micro germ but within a few days they became a mega deadly epidemic. From one mouth to the next they got stronger, uglier, nastier, crueler. So Master Calliga had no option but to find a quick fix, get rid of his youngest before it was too late. 'Cause in cases like this there was too late. Master Calliga knew it, Mrs. Calliga knew it, and the whole village of Artemis knew it. The only person who was in big denial was Zoë, the oldest daughter of the family who got really out of control when her baba announced Chrysa's wedding to the lawyer.

"Why? Why her?" she yelled and screamed, banging her heels on the wooden floor with anger.

"Just because," replied Master Calliga authoritatively.

"But why? I am the oldest. I should get married first," Zoë shouted once again.

"'Cause I said so," said the Master leaving Zoë in demonic delirium, fuming and shouting around the dining table with mega anger. The fumes reached Mrs. Calliga but Missus gave no better explanation to her daughter. So bitter feelings became more bitter and a day later Zoë found herself on her knees in front of GG's icon pleading for Divine help.

"Oh God, please don't let Chrysa marry the lawyer. Don't let baba dance in Chrysa's wedding before he dances in mine. Please God I beg you. I am your worshiper, remember? Remember me God? Remember me?"

Damn well I remember you, thought God glancing down at Zoë who was still whining in mezzo forte while getting ready to pull out her little notebook.

"Not again! That damn book," moaned God, releasing a not-so-Holy sigh.

But Zoë did as expected, pulled out her old tiny leathered notebook, opened it somewhere in the middle way and made a mark. Then she turned the page and started counting aloud. "one, four, seven, nine, eleven! Eleven! Eleven it is!" she yelled gladly looking at GG's icon. "You owe me eleven favors!" she added with enthusiasm. And after sending a sweet look at GG, she continued, "But I am willing to let them go. Just grant me this last wish and I will erase all your debts. All of them! One by one," Zoë added with a smile, sending her last meaningful look to GG. Then she stood up and went on with her daily life. GG was left alone wondering how she managed to end up with eleven. Based on His latest calculations nine was the closing number. Where the hell she got the extra two points, no one knew and no one was about to find out. GG wouldn't dare to dig into Zoë's notebook and Zoë wasn't in a mood to settle for anything less. As far as she was concerned her proposal to God was a gift from below, well worth the down stretch.

So for the next days Zoë buried her anger, her jealousy and any other non-sisterly feelings she had developed for Chrysa. She went even beyond expectations, helping Kyra Sophia clean up guest rooms, iron old lacy curtains, dust fine china and polish ancient family jewels.

"You see how Zoë is helping her little sister to get ready for her big day?" Mrs. Calliga started complaining to Sunday, the middle one who was wandering lazily around the kitchen, stealing sweets when Maro and Georgia weren't looking. And then, "Stop devouring whatever comes in front of you," Missus yelled furiously at Sunday, who seemed to pay little attention to her mama's remarks, masticating lethargically on a piece of sugarplum she had just taken from one of the many jars that belonged to Georgia. And a couple of days later, "You see my Zoë? How good and lovely sister she is?" Missus asked the Master when Zoë happily started spending endless hours at Madam Papadimou's atelier helping with Chrysa's wedding dress.

"A sister gotta do what a sister gotta do." That was Zoë's reply. A reply that was heard again and again over those days. A reply that became famous among servants and relatives and was used out of the blue in many occasions for many years to come. "A sister gotta do what a sister gotta do," said Maro to herself staring at Master Calliga's corpse many years later. "A sister gotta do what a sister gotta do," replied Pauper when Maro told him that the lawyer had deflowered his wife before him. "A sister gotta do what a sister gotta do," said Wicked Yiayia to my mama when my baba left our house.

And yes a sister gotta do what a sister gotta do, thought Zoë when she caught Chrysa in the middle of the night with a little suitcase in one hand and a plastic bag in the other trying to jump out of the bathroom window.

For a minute Chrysa stayed still, her eyes sparkling nervously through the dim candlelight trying to make out who was the person who was standing at the other end of the room. But as Zoë came closer, Chrysa realized that she had to act fast, so she threw her suitcase and her leg over the one side of the wall and the little bag on the other side. And puff! In no time Zoë found herself staring through a thick layer of red sauce wondering why the hell her sister was carrying a little plastic bag full of tomato pulp on the night of her mega rescue.

"Anyway, why the hell should I care?" questioned Zoë, washing the tomato sauce off her face minutes later. Then she walked quietly back to her room, laid between her flowery sheets and thanked GG silently for paying back His debts. What came next? Dreams! Bridal dreams. White, bright sugary dreams. And while Zoë was floating in pelagic happiness, dancing in the beat of Isaiah, her little sister Chrysa was making her way through the dark starless night.

Rehearsals Can Go So Far

We are all laying in the gutter, but some of us are looking at the stars.
—Oscar Wilde, *Lady Windermere's Fan*

An old big bicycle with no brakes and a lot of missing parts was agreed to be used for the mega rescue operation. Pauper would be the appointed driver, Dimitris the look out and the Key-holder the emergency back-up guy if things were to get out of hand. The operation was planned in full detail and rehearsed twice in Paradise. The first rehearsal was micro but real, like a military operation with little plastic solders on a piece of scribbled map. Calliga's Mansion was marked on one end of the bar with a bottle of Johnny Walker. Pauper's house was marked half a meter away with an empty beer-glass and streets and houses were spotted between with empty ouzo shots, turned upside down. A two-drachma coin was playing the role of the old heavy bike maneuvering through the upside down shots and leaving a slight but evident scratch on the wooden bar.

Dimitris held the bottle of Johnny Walker with both hands looking around in full alert. The Key-holder stood still on top of the empty beer-glass glancing nervously at the clock. Pauper rolled with his fingers the two-drachma coin from the empty beer-glass through the little ouzo shots and when he came fingers-to-face with Johnny he changed hands and rolled back with less speed and half maneuvering. When the coin reached its destination Pauper dropped it into the glass and shouted with enthusiasm, "Mission accomplished!"

The whole first rehearsal was done in full silence; meaningful looks were sent around a couple of times but no one dared to break the rigorous tone of the atmosphere. A suggestion was made a couple of minutes later but didn't go far. The Key-holder thought that Paradise was mismarked so he stretched his hand, picked up one of the little ouzo shots and replaced it with a peppershaker.

"Not that one!" Dimitris objected as soon as the Key-holder picked the little ouzo shot.

"You get my point now?" complained the Key-holder, "we gotta make sure what is what."

"The bike can't get through now," protested Pauper, dragging his hand between the peppershaker and a shot, pretending to roll the two-drachma coin.

"We gotta make it real, as real as it gets," added the Key-holder, this time louder, holding up the extra serious look.

"Let's roll it from the start," suggested Dimitris, but he was interrupted by the entrance of Fucking Auntie Puta. The three friends looked each other for a sec and without saying a word decided to dismiss the second rolling. So rehearsal No. One was officially over.

A day later rehearsal No. Two took place but that one was a paper rehearsal or, to be more precise, a napkin one, drawn by Dimitris on a piece of napkin after lunch. Two-mega olive oil stains were circled with blue ink on the napkin, the smaller one served as Pauper's house, the bigger one as Calliga's Mansion. A blue ink asterisk between the two oil stains was Paradise and random dots represented the rest of the houses. A curvy line going from one oil stain to the other and backwards marked the destination that Pauper's bike was to make. Three-fourths of the napkin-rehearsal survived, the last fourth was cut off by Dimitris and used as a gum wrapper when the Key-holder prohibited him to stick his used gum under the barstool he was sitting on. Below are the remains of the napkin-rehearsal

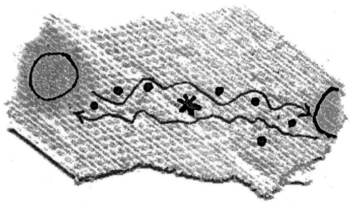

Hero and friends had plans to perform a couple more rehearsals but the plans got messed up so they arrived at the morning of the appointed day without much choice.

"You'll do fine. And don't forget we'll be there to help," Dimitris reassured Pauper patting him on the back.

"Definitely fine," added the Key-holder, smoking his cigarette and trying to hide his nervousness.

"Anyway real life is like a theater-play; rehearsals can only help so much," concluded Dimitris.

And right he was. Rehearsals can only help up to a certain point; beyond that a thousand things can go wrong. There might be an unexpected power cut and there goes your play. Or an accident; an actor might get sick or smashed and if that actor happens to be the primadona of your play you are fucked. Of course all those things are out of your hands, so you rehearse and hope for the best. And if the best comes you are set for success. If the best doesn't come, you along with your play end up in the gutter. And that's exactly where our hero and his loyal friends ended up while Chrysa was throwing her leg over Calliga's bathroom window. In the gutter. In the dry, shallow but wide gutter close to Paradise. In the same gutter that hosted Pauper's father a couple of weeks earlier. In that gutter that we'll all find ourselves some-day, some-time. But unluckily enough that day wasn't some-day. And that time wasn't some-time; it was exactly the day and the time planned for the mega rescue operation. How did they end up there? Well, that can't be answered in a simple short phrase. So let's back-up a bit and pick up where we left off—back to ouzo shot No. Four.

So what's after ouzo-shot No. Four? Ouzo-shot No. Five silly! And what's after ouzo-shot No. Five? Right you are! Ouzo-shot No. Six. And what's after ouzo-shot No. Six? You definitely got it right but Pauper, Dimitris, the Key-holder, Aromatist, Loo and the rest of the boys went into that foggy, blurry uncertain illusionary world that comes after the first half dozen of ouzo-shots so their mathematical abilities were out of hand. After ouzo shot No. Six, they stopped counting, thinking and behaving as sobers and started behaving like drunkards. And because they weren't everyday drunkards, lacking the experience and all, they were naïve enough to believe that when the time arrived they would be able to execute the rescue plan without much difficulty. So at twelve o'clock when mega heavy silence had covered the whole village of Artemis and most villagers were asleep, the old clock, which was hanging above Paradise's bar, started cuckooing.

"Cuckoo" and "cuckoo!"

"It's time," said Dimitris.

"Time?" questioned the Key-holder.

"Time flies," added Loo, gazing at the clock and trying to look more skeptical than drunk.

"Where to?" questioned Fucking Auntie Puta in giggles.

By the twelfth cuckoo Pauper was off his seat.

"The bike is in the back," yelled the Key-holder to Pauper and Dimitris who started walking slowly towards the front door.

"Just wait for me there," the Key-holder added and disappeared behind the bar. A few minutes later he arrived in front of Paradise dragging the old bike along his side.

"Let me give you a hand," said Dimitris to Pauper, who had just made an unsuccessful attempt to get on the bike.

"It'll be just fine," murmured the Key-holder as if he was talking to himself.

"Yeah, fine," agreed Pauper while raising his right leg clumsily.

"Butt on top of saddle," ordered Dimitris, and then, "There you go!" he shouted with great enthusiasm as if Pauper had just achieved something extraordinary. A few minutes later Dimitris was seating behind Pauper, his hands grabbing his friend's waist tightly, his legs hanging off each side of the bike like a pair of extra wheels.

"Get your legs off the ground," ordered Pauper, blinking his eyes a couple of times and trying to make out the road ahead.

"It's very dark," remarked the Key-holder, trying to focus his good eye, "maybe you need a flashlight."

"Nahh," yelled the two friends in one voice as the old big wheels started to squeak rolling slowly down the slope.

"See you in a flash," yelled the Key-holder with relief. And in a flash it was. Seconds later a weird clanging sound was heard and in the thick dark night you could hear several ahs and ohs. The Key-holder found his two friends in the bottom of the dry gutter. One next to the other. The front wheel of the old bike was on top of them while the second was still rolling down the hill in a great rush.

"What happened?" asked the Key-holder from above.

"The sky is full of stars," said Pauper with half open eyes.

The Key-holder turned his head and looked but saw nothing but a big moody sky. "Can't see a thing," he replied with disappointment.

"'Cause you aren't down here with us," said Dimitris bursting into a loud ceaseless laughter, pulling the Key-holder abruptly from his arm.

What Goes Around Comes Around

O n the morning of Chrysa's arranged wedding Mrs. Calliga, without even opening her eyes, placed her fingers where her right tit used to be and with slow, shy but steady moves started feeling the wounded area. Hoping for a bit of roundness, a little micro archiness, a tiny miniature of curviness. A mini miracle of science and Mrs. Calliga would have devoted herself to the power of reasoning, forgetting GG once and for all. After all, she had been gulping Puta's colorful jelly pills for thirteen days now. And today was the official deadline: if science had any intentions of making a move this was the day. The last and lucky day for science to prove itself and win the fight over GG. And of course science, being strong-minded and over-driven, wanted to be the winner. Shaking GG's superiority and monarchic nature even for a short period of time was science's life dream. But time was short. What could science do in thirteen days? Thirteen days might have been enough for GG, who had a million experiences in the miracle business, but for science thirteen days wasn't much. Obviously science was desperate for an extension but Mrs. Calliga wasn't going to hand it one. She herself didn't have much authority. The wedding was arranged: flowers, dresses, food, guests, they were all ready to take part in the mega ceremony and Missus couldn't do anything but grope for the best. And as she was groping a pretty unfamiliar bushy territory started tangling between her fingers. It was nothing like round, archy and curvy. This one was hairy, furry, and curly. It's one thing to wish for curvy and get curly (just a consonant micro mistake) and another thing to wish for round and archy and get hairy and furry. This was a mega mix-up. Once and for all science messed up big time leaving Mrs. Calliga furiously fingering through a wild land of curly hair.

"Oh my..." squealed Missus opening her eyes. And right away she ran in front of her full body mirror. For a second she stood there, eyeing her reflection, and her long time dead baba came into her mind. He had been a strong, tall, blue-eyed man with a long mustache and thick sideburns. For once the resemblance between him and his daughter was evident, but not in the color of their eyes or the wittiness of their smile. Unfortunately enough, it was in the thickness and darkness of their rich shiny hair.

"What a nightmare!" exclaimed Mrs. Calliga blinking her eyes with disbelief. But the mirror knew no tricks. Honestly and plainly the mirror reflected what was in front of it. Mrs. Calliga blinked and blinked and blinked for much more than the average blinking time and got exactly what she didn't desire; mega masculinity in all its hairiness. And since she had no time for whines, whimpers and the rest, she opened her drawer, got out a big pair of scissors and started trimming down the wildest bushiest areas of her body. Armpits came first; there was a lot of trimming there. Then the back of her knees. Then the area around her bellybutton. Then lower than that, the area around her womanly holy hole, which looked like a wild forest with high trees and top vegetation. And last but not least, her chest area. Mrs. Calliga started from left double D tit and as she were moving to the right her fingers froze, her anxious look started melting and a shy witty smile appeared on her face. "Why don't I leave it as it is?" she asked herself, looking down at her missing-tit hairy area. And then looking at the mirror, "Why don't I boost it up a bit?"

So she placed the pair of scissors on the bed and picked up a comb. Carefully she puffed up the new hair covering the wounded area as well as she could. A couple of minutes later she was proudly staring at a little bushy peak. Obviously it wasn't a fleshy new tit but surely it was a flashy new something. Big flat nothing was finally covered with something and Missus started feeling better. She gazed and gazed again and again. Much more was needed to balance the two sides but for a start things looked...well greatly hairy. So she smiled looking straight ahead. And her mustache smiled straight back at her. "I need something better for you," Missus said to the mustache and the mustache dropped its smiling curve at once. Missus put on her robe and headed for the bathroom. There after a quick search she found what she was looking for, her husband's razor. Sharp, long and shiny. "A thirsty bloody tool," she murmured, "cruel and brutal." And as she was getting emotionally ready to perform her first facial shaving, the Master's screaming voice interrupted her, "Womaaaan, womaaaan, come down."

What on earth, Missus thought, looking at the razor with hesitation.

"Woman!!!!! Where are you?" the Master yelled again, his heavy steps echoing on the wooden floor.

"In the bathroom," Missus shouted back and pressed the sharp edge on her upper lip.

"Cut the shit and come down here now," ordered the Master angrily.

"In a minute," shouted back Missus, slashing her mustache in half.

"No!!! I need you NOW!" yelled the Master louder.

Missus tried to ignore her husband's menace, came closer to the mirror and sheared off the rest of her mustache. Then she placed the razor in its case, freshened up her face with some cold water and exited the bathroom.

When she arrived at the living room she found her husband with a long piece of wood in his hands circling the living room table in mega fury.

"I am going to kill them, kill them with my bare hands," the Master was mumbling to himself again and again while moving the long piece of wood up and down.

"Kill who?" asked Missus indifferently.

"You and your daughter," yelled Master and with a jump came standing too close to his wife. He dropped the wood on the floor then grabbed Missus's left arm and while waving a piece of paper on top of her shiny upper lip, asked, "What's this? What the hell is this?"

Missus couldn't give him a better answer than the obvious. "Paper," she said.

"Smart ass! What is it?" yelled the Master once again while the edge of the paper touched Missus's silky upper lip.

"That's...that's my...my..." attempted Missus placing her free hand where her mustache used to be.

"Cut the fake hair," yelled the Master and Missus's eyes stretched widely at once.

I did, I did, she almost said, still gazing at the Master in mega astonishment.

"I want to know everything. I want to know what she means by this. I want to know whom I should kill first. How did she escape? From where did she leave?" yelled the Master in a blush.

"Jumped out the bathroom window," Zoë replied, entering the living room in an unusually refreshing mood.

Missus and the Master turned their heads at once, staring in mega awe.

Zoë, who immediately realized that she had talked too quickly, started fabricating a long string of fictional over-loose excuses. "Sometime, at

some point, somewhere I heard someone talking about Chrysa's escape."
When Zoë ran out of words, she focused at the paper, which the Master
was still holding in his hand and said,

"Don't look at me, just look here. Here is the answer."

It was then that Missus really focused on the piece of paper and
read,

"Dear baba & mama,

*I have decided to marry the man I love. You both must understand
and respect my decision. After all what goes around comes around.
Sometimes in a day!
Sometimes in more than a decade! Please forgive me.*

Your princess,

Chrysa."

As soon as Missus raised her gaze from Chrysa's letter, she felt her
legs' muscles weakening. Making an effort to regain her strength she
crossed her hands on top of her lap, sealed her dry lips tightly and stared
straight ahead. The word *princess* echoed in her mind loudly. Her legs
started shaking uncontrollably.

"Ohh, ohh, ohhhhh!!! I am going to faint," finally she whispered
and a sec later she tumbled onto the floor in front of her husband.

Current Era

A Polyglot Scene

I am home. And so are mama, Bo, his mama, George and Antonis. *A fucking mega gathering*, I think to myself as I walk in. The only one missing is Maria. Well, baba and Wicked Yiayia too but I stopped counting on baba's visits a long time ago and as far as Wicked Yiayia is concerned I don't dare wish for her unpleasant disruptions. Anyway I sense everybody's gaze burning on my face and I know that something mega has happened. Mama walks towards my side and with syrupy but melancholic tone starts the blah blah in motherly plain Greek.

"Κάθισε γλυκιά μου, έχει γίνει κάτι και πρέπει να δείξεις πόσο δυνατή είσαι," and immediately she corrects herself, "πόσο δυνατοί είμαστε."

Antonis and Bo exchange meaningful glances in universal language, only I grasp no meaning.

"Maria has slit her wrists," Bo's mama storms in and for a sec I can't make out the tongue she uses. The glances become distressing, shocking and fast, operating in pretty high speed.

"How?" I say and I immediately realize that I've just asked the most technical question in the most non-technical situation. But anyway that's the only one I am able to verbalize, at least for now.

"With her baba's blade," Antonis replies in English without looking at me.

"Where?" Technical question No. Two arrives in a rush. No language distinction here. Greek and English have immersed into one. I look at my pierced arm and think that pain is like music, it has no language boundaries.

"In the bathtub," Bo says.

A bloody similar bathroom scene from an American movie I watched over at George's house months ago comes into my mind. I don't recall its title but I remember the wrist slashing. What a mess! Blood, blood, blood! Everywhere. Juicy, thick, film type of blood. *Are our lives on the big screen too?* I ask myself in silence. A sec later I ask, "Why did she do it?"

"Αυτή είναι μια δύσκολη και περίπλοκη ερώτηση και τέτοιες ερωτήσεις έχουν και τις ανάλογες απαντήσεις," mama replies in an apologetic, justifying tone.

"Nah, there is nothing complicated about it," Bo rushes. "She got overworked at home with her baba and her mama and their splitting up situation, so she got into the bathtub and did what she did. It's a common scenario with common scenes. In America kids react like that pretty often. In America..." Bo goes on describing calmly the American dream in its everyday non-advertising version.

Americans have done it all for some time now. Americans are the pioneers. And now the exporters too! Good or bad their caca gets exported, spreading like butter on a piece of toast. *Anyway that's another fucking story*, I think and finally add, "My old folks went off too but I didn't slash my wrists."

"Everybody has his own reaction. Everybody is unique." Bo says and I think to myself *yeah yeah I know the famous slogan "Unique like everybody else!"* But before even attempting to verbalize my thought mama cuts me off abruptly.

"Η δικιά μας περίπτωση είναι διαφορετική. Ο πατέρας σου κι εγώ δεν χωρίσαμε. Έχουμε μικροδιαφορές αλλά είμαι σίγουρη ότι θα λυθούν πάρα πολύ σύντομα," she defends herself gazing anxiously around the room, looking for support that no one seems ready to provide.

Yours is a fucking denial case, I think. *Yours is the repetitive joke type; every time you say it, it gets better and better.* What really impresses me about mama is that she thinks that her situation is different from any other situation in this world. She believes that universal laws don't apply to her or any of her family members for that matter. Of course that's a Calliga trait and a Calliga trait is like a lethal genetic disease; you are born with it and die from it.

"Look, the good thing is that she didn't slash deep or enough, meaning she is still breathing. They took her to the hospital at Thessalonici. She isn't dead." Antonis answers the unspoken question in short cut phrases.

"As far as we know she isn't dead. She was breathing when they found her," explains Bo's mama, who seems to play the bad messenger's role with great success and extra self-control.

I take a deep breath, trying to focus on now and here and then ask when it happened and what we are to do.

"Τίποτα, η αλήθεια είναι ότι εμείς δεν μπορούμε να κάνουμε τίποτα," mama goes. Her reply doesn't shock me. She is always willing to do nothing, just wait for the *deus ex machina* to solve the problem and bring life back to normal.

"Tomorrow, tomorrow we should go to the hospital," George finally suggests as Bo, Antonis and I nod simultaneously.

Zoë, The Next Best Bride

How Chrysa's wedding dress fit Zoë was a mystery. A mystery that Master Calliga had neither time nor interest in resolving. But it was also a fact, a fact he was content to witness. Of course if things were a bit different the Master would have been more than just content, he would have been over-excitedly happy, after all he was getting rid of his oldest daughter along with twenty-three acres of his most infertile land. But things weren't different, so contentment was the highest the Master managed to reach on that day. But before reaching that state of simple contentment he went through an almost infinite and totally fruit-less bargain scene with the lawyer. The bargain started about six hours before the wedding, in other words as soon as Master Calliga announced to the lawyer that Zoë was going to be his great bride along with forty acres of his best land.

Reasonably enough, and more puzzled than ever, the lawyer asked, "Zoë? Why her?"

"She is better, hardworking and very disciplined, like a good wife ought to be," said the Master, trying to avoid the real cause of changing plans.

"But we agreed on Chrysa," protested the lawyer, looking even more confused than seconds earlier.

"Let's forget what we've said. Have my eldest. She is nice, goodhearted and makes the best mousaka in the whole northern part of Greece," added the Master looking at Zoë with pride and forcing a toothless smile.

"But I told everybody that I am marrying Chrysa," complained the lawyer.

"Who is everybody?"

"My friends, my relatives, people from the city, my...my..."

"Tell them you made a mistake. Zoë is better for you and she doesn't come empty handed. I am offering forty acres of my best land, that's the most fertile land in all of Greece, that's an offer no one can refuse, a lifetime opportunity," said the Master almost in one breath.

"Forty acres of land and her," repeated the lawyer skeptically and started walking around Zoë with steady slow steps and an over-examining eye. When he completed the first round he took a few steps backwards and stared at her for a couple of minutes.

As he was staring Mrs. Calliga took the opportunity to number her daughter's virtues one by one:

"1) Zoë is taller than Chrysa, 2) curvier, 3) extra mature, for her age that is, 4) she has a rich nature and great, great personality, 6) she is religious and has very good manners, 7) she is tidy and clean and 8)...8)... she...sheee..."

"She comes with forty acres of my best land," added the Master sending a shush-look to his wife. The lawyer did and said nothing; still his eyes were nailed on Zoë's frozen body. After a few seconds of full, heavy silence the Master walked closer to the lawyer, patted him on the back and added, "There is no need for us to pinpoint the obvious, you take what you see; a well nurtured girl from the best family around, the Calliga family, it can't get better than that. Can it? Can it?" he repeated without really expecting a reply. But as always the unexpected arrived in an arithmetic rush.

"A hundred!"

"A hundred?" questioned the Master sending his wondrous gaze from left to right.

"A hundred acres of land," replied the lawyer in mega staccato, his face showing no expressive indications of any type.

"A hunddreed!!! One zero zero???" went slowly but very loudly the Master while his right thumb and pointer were demonstrating the numbers in front of his over stretched eyes.

"But she is a curvy girl," jumped in Missus who sensed that her husband was on the verge of a mega breakdown.

"Curvy but in the wrong places," the lawyer finally replied, focusing on Zoë's big flat butt.

Zoë, who had neither moved nor talked till that moment, arched her back at once, mega rear protruding from left and right, its flat cheeks looking flatter and more endless than ever, manipulating the colorful floral patterns of her jersey dress beyond limits.

"Obviously the eye fails to see hidden beauties," added Missus with a proud tone, glaring at the lawyer from the lower corner of her eye.

"Obviously the beauty is in the eye of the beholder," replied the lawyer.

"Obviously enough is enough," shouted the Master and immediately added, "fifty's my final offer."

"Eighty!" yelled back the lawyer.

"Sixty!" the Master.

"Seventy-five!" the lawyer.

"Seventy!" the Master.

"Seventy-five!" insisted the lawyer once again.

But this time there was no reply, at least not a verbal one. Just a finger-snap followed by a finger-arrow pointing at the main door. Obviously the Master had neither words nor numbers left.

"Snap-snap," his strong callused fingers went once again and then his forefinger tenaciously, quickly and steadily pointed at the main exit. Missus's expression changed at once; surprise in its largest size and brightest colors sat upon her face and didn't seem to have plans of moving any time soon. Zoë's worried gaze jumped desperately from the Master to Missus while her butt was swinging in opposite directions. The lawyer, who didn't comprehend the Master's reaction immediately, looked around and then said in a half affirmative, half questionable tone, "Seventy five!?"

At that very moment the Master went back to his verbal mode and started yelling repeatedly, "Get out of my house, get out of my house, out, out, out." The lawyer picked up his jacket and got lost behind the big slamming door without saying a word.

Groom No 2

If you've got him by the balls his heart and mind will follow.
—John Wayne

Unfortunately, the Master Calliga didn't manage to grab the lawyer by his balls, so the lawyer bolted. Of course the Master knew that grabbing someone's balls is not an easy job and when that someone happens to be a lawyer the grabbing gets even harder. So he didn't regard his failure as mega. But on the other side of the room were standing Mrs. Calliga along with Zoë who had a totally different interpretation of the matter. In Mrs. Calliga's and Zoë's eyes the Master's failure was huge, gigantic, mega, the extra extra extra large size, the one found only in America. Therefore, after the lawyer's exit things progressed instantaneously: Mrs. Calliga collapsed and Zoë panicked. The collapsing was small and short. It happened in a splash. "SLAM," the main door went and "PUFF," Mrs. Calliga fell back on the big ancient armchair, which happened to be behind her. That was the second collapsing for that day. After Mrs. Calliga's collapsing arrived Zoë's panicking which was neither small nor short but rather mega and pretty long, in high volumes and extravagant gesticulations.

"For five acres? I lost him for five acres? 'Cause my baba doesn't care for me, 'cause he only cares for his damned land, 'cause he is an egoist, 'cause I am an unlucky child, 'cause God...God...God..." went Zoë hesitating to come up with an accusation for God whom as far as she knew had kept His promises to His best.

"Five acres!!!! Five damned acres and he would have agreed to marry me," Zoë continued her hollering while her hands were flying in opposite directions.

The Master couldn't remember the last time he saw Zoë in such delirium. And he couldn't remember simply because this was Zoë's first mega panicking act. Of course as a normal every day type of daughter she had undergone a couple of freaking out situations, but she had never before reached such a terrifying frightening condition. It wasn't really what she was saying and the high tone of her voice that alerted the Master but the way she was looking at him; her eyes shrunk, her pupils glittered, staring murderously straight into his eyes. It was a horrifying scene.

Looking at Zoë the Master remembered what the mayor had told him a long time ago; women come in three types: the type who kills for love, the type who kills for marriage, and the type who kills for food. Obviously Zoë belonged in the second category, while Chrysa and Sunday in the first and third. "God has blessed me with all three types," the Master murmured to himself, making an effort to focus on the bright side of the situation. But in vain. Zoë's demonic delirium was growing furiously fast. Now she placed her flat butt on the floor and started wriggling her body in the middle of the room like a fish out of the water while bouncing her fists violently on the wooden floor.

"You are the reason for my misfortune, my suffering, my misery," she yelled again and again, nailing her baba with her evil gaze.

Missus, who was just coming out of her brief collapsing, stared at Zoë in confusion. In her opinion the reason for Zoë's misfortune, suffering and misery wasn't the Master but the humiliation, which was about to come upon the Calliga family once the bad news spread around the village. If there was a way to stop the upcoming humiliation, Missus would have cared less for Zoë's misfortune. If her family name wasn't in any danger, Missus would have just gone to her room, gulped some of Puta's colorful pills and fallen into a long deep peaceful sleep. Anyway, she was feeling over-tired, extra exhausted, drained inside out. But ifs were far from reality, so she gathered up all her strength and stood up on top of Zoë, who was still mopping the floor with her big butt.

"Who is going to marry me now? Who is going to marry me?" Zoë's voice echoed from one side of the room to the other.

Missus glanced at her husband for a sec. When she realized that Zoë had managed to frighten even her own baba, she took a good look around and after a brief pause replied, "the Key-holder. The Key-holder will marry you."

"What?" said Zoë and Master at once.

"The Key-holder," Missus repeated once more in an almost convincing tone.

"What Key-holder?" questioned Zoë as she was getting her butt off the floor.

"The Paradise's Key-holder," said Missus with confidence.

At that very moment the door opened and Kyra Sophia walked in.

"The Key-holder wants to see Master," announced Kyra Sophia and the Master's and Zoë's eyes expanded in all directions.

"Please tell him to come right in," replied Missus happily, "and bring some ouzo." For a sec Kyra Sophia hesitated. Then she looked at Missus, gathered her courage and asked, "Paradise's owner, you know who I am talking about, right?"

"Of course. Of course. We have been waiting for him," Mrs. Calliga assured her, sending a meaningful look to her husband.

"All right then," replied Kyra Sophia skeptically.

"Can you give me a sec?" said Zoë, who seemed to have just comprehended her mama's plan.

"Actually, treat him with some ouzo and then bring him in. That will give my Zoë plenty of time. Right sweetie?" asked Missus with a big smile.

"Right, right," agreed Zoë blinking her eyelids with charisma.

Ten minutes later the Key-holder entered the Calliga's living room and received warm welcomes, big smiles, extra large sardines and so many ouzo shoots that he got confused, dizzy and was unable to remember the purpose that brought him to the Aristocratic Mansion in the first place. Kyra Sophia, who had plenty of strong memory, a focused mind, mega persistence, and avoided any type of alcohol during the morning hours, made several attempts to remind him of the nature of his visit but had no success. The Master, Missus and Zoë were all over him, pampering him physically, emotionally and mentally.

The whole scene was beyond comprehension, aristocratic in its greatest. So when an hour later Master Calliga stated that he would be delighted to have a man like him as his son-in-law, the statement didn't seem as coming out of nowhere. On the contrary, it seemed natural, logical, normal. The Key-holder was flattered, over flushed and feeling as if he was just given an extra pair of balls. And a man with four balls doesn't think as the ordinary every-day male type, meaning part time with his lower brain and part time with his upper. A man with four balls is a full time ball thinker, in other words an empty-headed jerk. So by the end of that visit the Key-holder promised: 1) to marry Zoë at that very afternoon, 2) to hand Paradise's key to a relative of his trust and 3) to become a full time manager/worker on Calliga's most infertile piece of land. Immediately after, he was sent home in order to get prepared for promise No. One, the cursed wedding, as it became known later on.

Surprise! Surprise!

As Zoë was trying to get into Chrysa's wedding dress, at the other end of the town Chrysa was getting out of bed. It was almost one in the afternoon. Pretty late for a bright bride of her type or any bride of any type for that matter. But Chrysa had an excuse for oversleeping and her excuse was like an old walnut tree; mega, solid and well grounded. Hangover! Yes, she had a hangover. As a matter of fact it wasn't really her hangover but Pauper's hangover. How was it possible that Pauper's hangover got into Chrysa? Well, based on Olga's beliefs if love is in the air, anything is possible. And love was in the air; that's why the air wasn't feeling its usual self but sticky, smelly and heavy-headed.

So in that cranky air Chrysa opened her eyes, looked around, and questioned herself.

Where am I?

Precisely where you deserve honey, herself replied sarcastically as Chrysa started rubbing her eyes tenaciously.

But everything looks so crammed! Chrysa whined sleepily.

It doesn't look crammed, IT IS CRAMMED! Herself shouted back.

I can't breathe! Chrysa continued.

You can, you can, just get your damned hands off your face, herself replied once again.

But there is not enough air in this room, Chrysa complained.

There is plenty of air, you little spoiled Calliga brat, continued herself, this time with extra sarcasm and mega irony.

And as internal chit-chat was warming up Chrysa's lungs, her face got from pink to red from red to redder, from redder to beet and from beet to beetter.

Olga, who all this time was massaging the still tender area around her tailbone, stood up, came closer to Chrysa and asked, "You are awake!? Good, good. And how do you feel, my little sister?"

That latest characterization was Olga's way of welcoming Chrysa into the family but Chrysa didn't catch the warm salutation, at least not at first. So with an annoying tone in her voice she replied, "I have an upset stomach, a huge headache and an over dry tongue."

Olga came even closer to Chrysa, studied her face for a sec and then asked, "How about your consciousness?"

"What do you mean, my consciousness?" wondered Chrysa, lifting herself up on one elbow.

"I mean your consciousness. Do you feel a small burden, a light guilt, a tiny little fear?"

"Burden, guilt, fear," mumbled Chrysa in confusion and then added skeptically, "Now that you mentioned it I think I do, I do feel a bit guilty."

"Then it's a hangover. You got a hangover," Olga assured her while heading for the sink.

"You should drink water, lots of water, and you'll be fine," she added, and a minute later she handed Chrysa a full glass of water.

Chrysa drank it at once. When she finished she looked Olga straight in the eyes and asked, "What's a hangover?"

"It's like goose bumps, only your skin crawls from inside. You get it when you drink too much alcohol."

"But I haven't drunk any alcohol," objected Chrysa.

"But my brother has and you love my brother, right? Right?" questioned Olga with anxiety.

Chrysa lowered her eyes and said nothing.

"It's okay. It's okay," Olga went on in her usual sweet low tone. Then she placed half of her butt on the edge of the bed, took Chrysa's hands in hers and said, "Love is magical, miraculous, mysterious and most of all capable of anything. When there is love anything is possible, everything is manageable, all is acceptable, nothing is unachievable and any, any pain is bearable."

Olga's words weren't really Olga's words. They were words she had managed to dig up from the romance book Betty Mulatto, her friend in America, had given her before leaving. The title of that book was *The Faces of Love* and Olga had spent almost the entire previous night facing the ceiling with her rear while reading again and again what she thought were the most perfect, extra romantic passages. She was reading 'cause she was unable to sleep. You see this was the fourth day after her accident at Paradise, the day she stopped taking painkillers. So her drowsiness was gone and in its place came alertness with a touch of thrill and a thick garniture of excitement. Of course drowsiness-less wasn't her only reason for being unable to sleep. There were also reason No. Two and reason No. Three. Reason No. Two was that she was in love with the Key-holder and eager to get totally well and fall in his arms forever and ever. And reason

No. Three today was the day of the big surprise. Today Olga was going to offer 200,000 drachmas to Pauper and Chrysa as their wedding gift. YES you read right! There is no arithmetic mistake here. Olga was going to give 200,000 drachmas to her brother and Chrysa. And YES you do remember correctly, that's Olga's entire life savings. How did she go from 100,000 drachmas to 200,000 drachmas? Well, several things contributed to the augmentation of the amount but the most important and main contributor was love; the boiling hot, velvety red and infinitely massive type. Remember?

So while Olga was reciting her bibliographical erotic expertise to Chrysa with zeal and zest Chrysa had time to let her eyes wander around the room. And because the wandering was very short and very brief, Chrysa asked, "Is your brother in the other room?"

"What other room?" questioned Olga, and after a micro pause, "There is no other room. This, thiiissss is our house," added Olga dragging the second *this* beyond limits.

"Ehhh...ehhh..." went Chrysa while at the back of her head she was trying to convert Olga's answer into meters and centimeters.

"If there is love, a thousand good souls can fit in a room," said Olga, patting Chrysa's shoulder.

"Five by six, five by seven?" mumbled Chrysa between her teeth skeptically.

"A thousand, a thousand good souls, that's what they say, right?" said Olga in an ecstatic tone looking into Chrysa's eyes tensely.

Unfortunately, Chrysa wasn't counting souls but bodies and as much as she counted and recounted, she was unable to fit more than say three or four bodies of a reasonable size into a five by six or maybe five by seven meter room. *For one thing, where does everybody sleep?* Chrysa wondered in her mind. *And then, there are only two beds and a love seat. And where is the bathroom? There is no other door than the one I got in last night. Is this a house? Is this my beloved's house?*

Olga wasn't able to sneak into Chrysa's mind but she was able to sense that something wasn't quite right. So she focused on Chrysa's eyes and asked, "Is everything all right, my sister?"

"I am just...just...hmm..." Chrysa mumbled as she started straightening her messy hair with her fingers.

"I'll take care of that," jumped Olga grabbing her purse. In a sec she took out her comb and started combing Chrysa's long shiny hair with care. As soon as she finished, she took out her brightest red lipstick and pressed it on Chrysa's lips. "Here you go. Now you are ready to look love straight in the eye," she said cheerfully. Then she opened a little golden mirror and held it in front of Chrysa's face. When Chrysa looked at her reflection her demeanor turned upside-down in a sec, just like that. A mega festivity with loud music, lots of wild dancing and infinite booze would have given a precise description of what went on in Chrysa's head for the next couple of seconds. After blinking more than a dozen times, she turned around, stared at the red lipstick which Olga was still holding in her hands and mumbled something totally incomprehensible.

Olga, who was accustomed to foreign parlance, pumped up her chest with as much air as possible and announced proudly, "You see how a bit of color can change everything. You see? You see?" Obviously she wasn't aiming for a reply, she just wanted to emphasize her gigantic ability of turning any unpleasant situation into picture-perfect. And since Chrysa was far from grasping the obvious, Olga decided to go on.

"So, my little sister, you see how a pair of red lips can brighten our perspective? I am telling you the magic is in small things, it comes in tiny micro packages. So this red lipstick is yours. Really it's all yours. And now I have another small MEGA surprise for you," Olga announced ecstatically. Then she reached underneath the bed, grabbed a rectangle brown paper bag and placed it on Chrysa's lap.

"Here is your wedding gift," she added, "I was planning to give it to you once my brother gets here, but there is no need to wait. Anyway women manage the family's money and since you are going to be my brother's wife I thought… well, here you go, go on open it."

Chrysa took the package into her hands and tried not to look curious.

A sec later the rubber band holding the brown paper bag flew at the other end of the room. Two hundred one-thousand-drachma bills spread on the bed as Chrysa's eyebrows reached hairline borders.

"Surprise! Surprise!" exclaimed Olga with mega satisfaction standing proudly next to Chrysa.

And "Surprise!? Surprise!?" muttered Chrysa staring from bills to lipstick and vice versa.

G Spot (for Georgie)

(Sorry Grafenberg nothing to do with you!)

While Chrysa was stretching her eyes beyond limits in front of Olga's poly-drachmic bills, four houses away the widow was stretching her legs in front of Pauper's face. Today was not a fucking day. Today was an educational day. The widow had promised to reveal the deepest, hottest, most sensitive secret of the female kind to Pauper and Pauper had promised to be totally, fully and solely mentally erect. Of course being totally, fully and solely mentally erect in front of a pair of rosy moist vaginal lips isn't an easy job but Pauper was determined to overcome any primitive impulses and go beyond usual fucking fucks. He was doing it in the name of love. So unsurprisingly enough the name of love was going through his mind as his fingers were going through the widow's flaming lips.

"G for...for... golden?" he asked the widow with a big smile on his face.

"Nah, it's G for Georgie," the widow explained while pressing her fingers on top of his.

"For Georgie?" questioned Pauper with disappointment and mega confusion.

"Yeah, my Georgie was the first to land a hand on it. He was the mega discoverer. He was the one who found it, woke it up and from that day on I was a different woman; a whole woman, if you know what I mean," stated the widow with mega pride and a huge smile.

"But this is your spot, your Georgie's spot, my Chrysa's spot can't be Georgie's spot. Can it?" objected Pauper, raising both eyebrows.

"Of course, of course," agreed the widow, "that can't be Georgie's spot. I wouldn't allow it anyway. I want my Georgie's soul and body to rest in peace, as it has been all these years. God took him from me when I was only eighteen. He had just turned twenty. We were less than three months married when he was killed. From that day on I've been looking for his warm hug all over. But you know what? There is no hug like Georgie's. No hug like his. Ahh my Georgie, my Georgie!" the widow said nostalgically with a sigh.

Pauper gazed around without knowing what he was supposed to say or do. This was the first time he was bending in front of the widow and his tsootsoo wasn't making any moves, just resting in his trousers in deep mega sleep. This was the first time he was really looking at the widow. She was in her early forties. Her face was like a cracked porcelain vase, beautiful but old and tired. Her opened legs were full of bluish lingering veins, her breasts spread wide as if they were avoiding facing each other. Only her eyes looked young and fresh, like the eyes of a little innocent girl, dark brown sparkling anxiously, curiously, fearlessly.

"Ahh my Georgie!" the widow sighed once again and placed both hands on top of Pauper's which were still groping through her flaming vaginal lips.

"So you are right, let's call Chrysa's G spot golden, anyway she is golden and that's the core of her goldenness," added the widow. Then she put on her serious instructive face and went on.

"As I told you every woman has her own G spot and every good husband ought to discover it. You know what they say?" she asked Pauper.

Pauper turned his head towards the ceiling and paused. He had no fucking idea what she was talking about but he didn't want to look as if he was out of the loop so he put on his skeptical face and stared at the ceiling. The widow smiled, brushed her fingers through his golden straight hair and said, " It's okay if you don't know. You don't have to pretend. Anyway today is my day. Today I am supposed to tell you all the secrets for a good loving lasting life. You just have to take notes. Just watch and feel. So where was I?" she asked herself and then, "Ah!! They say that a good husband is a good breadwinner but a great husband is a great G-spotter. And I bet you wanna be both; a good breadwinner and a great G-spotter. Right?" she asked with a smile.

Pauper nodded. Certainly he wanted to be a great husband. That's the reason he agreed to put his head between the widow's legs in the first place. That's the reason he had decided to dedicate his whole afternoon to education. Education is preparation for life and a man's education is more important than anything else. That was his opinion on the matter and he was prepared to do anything to educate himself.

"Now go on. Rub it," the widow ordered him, placing her pointer on top of Pauper's middle finger.

"No, not like that. Circularly! There are no ins and outs here, just gentle spherical moves. G spots are like full moons; full moons are fully illuminated by the direct sunlight, waiting for the eastern sun to rise with the movement of gentle fingers."

"That's good. Bravo! Bravo!" she exclaimed and immediately added, "just like that, ummm!! Go on. Don't stop now. You are doing fine." She sighed, stretching her body and smiled with satisfaction.

Pauper was in big mental concentration, almost breathless, kneeling between the widow's legs and moving his finger as instructed. A good, obedient student.

"Here it comes! Ahhh!!! Ohhh!!! You are an angel," the widow said finally with a smooth velvety tone in her voice.

"Once you find her golden spot you are set for life. Nothing can go wrong after that," she added and pulled Pauper's hand off her. Then she sat on the bed, and as she started buttoning up her robe she asked, "Now my boy, do you have any questions?"

Pauper looked at his wet fingers as if he wanted to say something, but hesitated.

"What is it? What's the matter?" she asked.

"Well, that's that's your... your...your doing," he finally managed to say still eyeing at his wet fingers.

"Well, yeah that's my doing but that's after your magical doing," she replied with a furtive look. Pauper's face went from skeptical to surprise and vice versa. The widow stood up, placed her hands on her waist and said with a playful tone in her voice, "What do you think? Only men pour their stuff into women? Ejaculation is solely a masculine act? Women don't contribute into the erotic pulp? Well, let me tell you, my boy, without women's contribution babies would come out sad, unhappy, gloomy, moody without real purpose in life, if you know what I mean."

Pauper didn't know what the widow meant but he wasn't ready to admit his ignorance. Until that moment he had considered himself a pretty experienced mega *jumper*. And in a way he was. He had been doing it for years. The widow was his first, then came a gypsy, later on the gypsy's daughters and just a day ago the Asian whore. Okay, he had to pay for doing it but at the time no decent girl was going to spread her legs before going to the church and no decent man was going to marry her once he had had her. An easy catch was for having fun, not for family and babies. That was the local law and Pauper had been a lawful citizen.

So he sent an apologetic gaze to the widow, wiped his hand with one edge of the sheet and said, "I am sorry I didn't mean to offend you."

"It's okay. Don't worry," said the widow and kissed his forehead. "Just remember, the first time is not about G spots, the first time is about being patient, smooth, sweet. Use all the pros we talked about and everything will be fine. Go on now. And good luck with your married life," she added, looking straight into his eyes.

Pauper hid his nose into her boobs, took a deep breath, and patted her rear with both hands.

"Goodbye, my Madonna," he said as he was exiting the house.

"Ciao, my boy," said the widow and blew him a kiss.

"Fucking yellow balls, that's the end of that," Pauper said to himself once he was outside the house. Then he combed his hair with his fingers, exhaled deeply and headed for Paradise. He was eager to talk to the Keyholder, who that very morning went to see Master Calliga in order to convince him to accept Pauper as his son-in-law.

Current Era

Second-Hand Thoughts

We arrive at the hospital. Maria is lying on the metal-framed bed; her face pale, her vague gaze floating around the room without purpose, her long body looking fragile and longer than ever, her wrists neatly wrapped in white gauze. Her mama is seated next to her but as soon as Bo, George, Antonis and I enter she stands up and exits the room dipped in mega tears and heavy silence. We are left behind, standing in a perfect semi-circle for a few seconds. Then Bo goes closer to the bed and aims for eye contact.

"Hey," he says.

"Hey," she goes as if she's just noticed us.

"What's up?" he asks.

"What's up with you?" she replies with a smooth lingering smile.

"What's up with us?" Bo says looking at George, Antonis and me.

The conversation is going nowhere and everywhere. The repetition makes the air unbreathable. This is how friends react after an unsuccessful suicide attempt. This is how words get trapped when emotional pressure gets above normal levels.

"How do you feel?" asks Antonis.

"Great, great," goes Maria, smiling melancholically and showing off her wrists.

"You'll be fine," I say, coming closer.

"Babe, sooner or later we'll all be fine," she replies cunningly.

160

"Better be sooner 'cause later I won't be around to witness it," goes Bo.

"You are leaving us, man?" asks Maria while studying my face, looking for some kind of reaction and ending up with nothing.

"In less than a week, so you better get out of that bed pretty soon," Bo says, gazing at me.

"I'll get out now," Maria goes as she pulls up her body.

"Well, we can wait a day or two. It doesn't have to be today. It doesn't have to be now," replies George to Maria and then turns to Bo, Antonis and me. "Right guys?"

"Right, definitely right," I add, trying to be convincing, trying to look mirthful.

"What's wrong with now? Now is better than tomorrow. Haven't you heard that saying? *If you can do something now, don't leave it for later,*" Maria says as she lets her long legs hang off the bed.

"I thought that here, in Greece, everything is left for later," says Bo.

"We cannot take you with us," goes George to Maria slowly.

"You are not taking me with you, I am leaving," she replies in similar slow motion. Then she looks at me and orders, "Pass me my clothes. They are hanging behind the door."

I am not sure what to do. So I look around, trying to gain time, hoping for a rescue.

Maria gathers all her strength, stands up and orders me once again, "Get my jeans." Then she takes off the white hospital gown and, nude, she eyes us with an eager look.

For minutes our bodies make no moves. The whole conversation is done with our eyes. Angry, unsettled, pleading gazes start to steam up the room in no time. *Am I being a sissy once again?* I question myself silently. I want to hug Maria, cover her naked body with my hands. For the first time I feel ashamed of her nudity. I feel ashamed of our nudity. I don't want to feel ashamed, that's the last thing I want to feel. After all it's their mistake she is standing in the middle of a hospital room like this. It's their mistake we are here. It's them who didn't keep up with their promises, letting their dreams fall short. How long will we have to pay for their mistakes? I wonder in my mind while looking at Maria's body. Then I sense George's imposing gaze over my shoulder and, as if a greater force conquers my soul, I reach behind the door, grab Maria's jeans and T-shit, and throw them over.

Bo, Antonis and George turn and stare at me with surprise. Maria smiles with satisfaction as she bends over to pick up her clothes.

"I am not getting involved in this," George announces in a dull slow motion.

"How will you get out of here without them noticing you?" Antonis asks.

"They don't give a fuck. Really, do you think they give a fuck?" Maria replies as she tucks in her t-shirt.

"They don't give a fuck for important stuff but for micro fucking details like this they do. They have spent their whole lives focusing on micro fucking details; they are detail-experts. Haven't you learned yet?" I say while trying to plot a rescue plan in the back of my head.

"Sunday is right," Antonis agrees, and then, "if you've decided to leave we should think before acting."

"WE? WE should think?" George protests once again, "I am out of this. I am not kidnapping a sick person from the hospital."

"We aren't asking for your help," I reply without looking.

"Stay cool guys," adds Maria. "I don't want you to fight over me. Really I can make it out of here without your help, just jump out the window. It's not high. It's just a micro jump. Don't forget, they might be experts in fucking up our lives but I am an expert in fucking up, literally the old good common way, if you know what I mean," Maria says smiling, showing off her shiny perfectly aligned teeth.

And it happens as she says. As George, Antonis, Bo and I exit the room one by one calmly, melancholically, she jumps out the window. Minutes later we meet her in the hospital's backyard. No one notices a thing. And least for now.

Ancient Era

A Sweet End

We aren't what we eat. We are what we don't shit.
—Hugh Romney, *Diet for a New America*

The night that Chrysa lost her virginity for the second time, her sister Sunday lost her life. She was twenty years old. A virgin. She knew nothing about love, hate, jealousy or pain, but lots about food. Eating she loved and from eating she died. Sweets were her specialty, she devoured them in handfuls. The day of Zoë's wedding Sunday ate thirty-two loukoumades, four pieces of baklava, six pieces of the wedding cake, seventeen dark chocolate truffles, forty-nine sugared almonds, four pieces of Kataifi, eight sesame cookies, three pieces of pasta flora and two plates filled with yogurt, honey and nuts. When the last guests were leaving, Sunday rushed to the bathroom. That was time No. Five.

"Come on, get out!" she yelled. She squeezed and squeezed but her rear exit had jammed hours ago. "Shit," she murmured but shit she didn't see.

That same night as she was laying on her bed in mega deep sleep, her belly gave up like an over stuffed grape leaf torn right in the middle. There was more food on that bed than on any villager's dinner table. Sunday was a mountain of sweetness. And sweetness filled everybody's memory every time her name came up in conversations. Of course that was outside the Calliga Mansion. Inside there was silence and guilt in their largest sizes and darkest colors. After the funeral Sunday's name was never spoken within the Calliga walls. Tons of guilt accumulated on Mrs. Calliga's shoulders. Stacks of blame filled Zoë's subconscious. The Master cursed and screamed, "Chrysa, Chrysa is responsible for this. If she hadn't run away with that filthy low creature none of this would have happened." Kyra Sophia was speechless, sunk in deep sadness. She had warned them of the upcoming misfortune.

"When a mirror breaks, expect seven years of bad luck. When a wedding dress is worn by another bride expect a death in the family," she told the Master and Missus when she saw Zoë wearing Chrysa's wedding dress.

"Nonsense, get out of here," the Master yelled.

"If our family's name is humiliated then we'll ALL be dead. Do you want that to happen, Sophia?" Mrs. Calliga asked her.

"You know what I want," replied Kyra Sophia calmly and then, "You can see both of your daughters in white; Chrysa and Zoë. It's your call, give Chrysa your blessing and have both weddings the upcoming weekend, no rush," added Kyra Sophia but the Master went furious. He didn't want to hear a word about Chrysa. As far as he was concerned Chrysa wasn't his daughter. She wasn't a Calliga. Not anymore.

Unfortunately, the Calliga couple had the opportunity to see both of their daughters in white. One that same day at the church and the other a day later at her own funeral. Chrysa's wedding dress went from Zoë to Sunday in less than twenty-four hours.

Chrysa witnessed her sister's funeral from a distance. Pauper, Olga, Fragile and Dimitris were standing next to her. Chrysa wept for Sunday, Olga for the Key-holder, and Fragile for Kyra Vana who was still missing. Pauper and Dimitris stared motionless. When they all returned home Chrysa had a huge appetite: she finished two full plates of spaghetti and had an irresistible crave for sweets.

"An exhausting day, she had," murmured Olga to Fragile, who was staring at Chrysa in great shock.

Later that night Pauper announced to Chrysa that he was going to buy a house. It was Olga's idea but Pauper presented it as his.

"We can't live here in one room, we need space. Soon we are gonna have kids. They'll need their own room," he said gazing at Chrysa's tearful face. He was in love as never before. The whole day he played and replayed in his mind their lovemaking scene from the previous night. He wasn't sure if he had discovered her golden spot but anyway *the first time is not about G spots, the first time is about being patient, smooth and sweet.* And he had tried his best. He placed a big pillow underneath Chrysa's butt and then made his entrance as smoothly as he could. He didn't rush. *A slow smooth in and slow smooth out,* the widow's words echoed in his head as he was trying to keep the right tempo. Of course when he reached the peak point, education was dropped, rules were forgotten and ins and outs came and went in their own wild rhythm.

When he was done, he kissed Chrysa on the lips, pulled himself out very carefully and laid next to her without saying a word. Was any blood on the pillow? On the sheets? Between Chrysa's thighs? He didn't know. It was too dark to see anyway. "Good night," Chrysa murmured shyly. "Good night," he replied and felt asleep within minutes.

The next day he rushed out of bed when he heard Kyra Sophia's cries. She had come to announce Sunday's death. Pauper held Chrysa in his arms and told her the bad news. Chrysa curved her trembling body against his and burst into tears. Pauper's heart was torn into a thousand pieces. He didn't know what to do. No lessons would have prepared him for that.

Love hurts so much, he remembered Olga saying.

"Patchouli, patchouli," suggested Fragile, "when my husband died only the smell of patchouli calmed me down." But when Pauper sprayed some patchouli in the room, Chrysa's stomach turned upside down. She couldn't stop throwing up.

Olga, who had just picked up the sheets and pillows from Chrysa's and Pauper's bed and was about to go outside to hang them, looked at her brother's desperate eyes and without much thought she ordered him, "here take these and go outside. I'll take care of Chrysa."

For a sec Pauper didn't move. He was surprised. "What am I supposed to do?" he questioned in silence, staring at the sheets and pillows, which Olga has just placed on his lap.

"Leave her to me, come on go outside," said Olga once again, sending him a meaningful look. Pauper hugged the sheets and pillows with relief and exited the room. A few seconds later his cheeks started burning as a toothless smile sat on his face. "My love," he murmured staring at one of the pillows, which looked like a Picasso unfinished sketch at the beginning of his Rose Period. Then he brought the pillow close to his nose and took a deep sniff.

"Even your blood smells good," he mumbled squeezing pillows and sheets against his chest. Apparently he was too involved in his daydreaming or whatever that was to notice when seconds later Olga's red lipstick slipped off the cluster of wrinkled sheets and started rolling from one side of the balcony to the other. By the time Olga's lipstick reached one of the balcony corners, Pauper had hanged the sheets on the yellow rope and with the pillows still squeezed against his chest entered the room.

Then he saw Olga squeezing Chrysa's hands in hers as she had done three nights earlier when Pauper and Dimitris were laying in the gutter, totally drunk. Then Olga was acting for love's sake, now for death's sake.

"My little sister cry, cry. It's okay," Olga said as Chrysa's tears were rolling ceaselessly down her face. It was the first time that Olga was following no bibliographical instructions. The first time that Betty's Mulatto romance books seemed totally useless. All of a sudden Olga knew what to do and she was doing it with confidence, as if she had tons of experience. Three days later Olga announced to Chrysa that she wasn't planning to go back to America.

"As I was holding you a voice shouted in my head: Your home is here, Olga. Here! There is no need to run away anymore," Olga confessed to Chrysa.

"So you'll be my sister?" Forever?" Chrysa asked anxiously. And Olga smiled.

Chrysa and Olga lived like sisters until three years later on September 25, 1966, when Olga had her third and last accident. She was killed instantly by a tractor in the fields. She had gone to collect red poppies for Pauper's and Chrysa's upcoming anniversary. That same afternoon Kyra Vana returned home. She entered the single-room house as she had exited it three years earlier; same canvas bag over her shoulder, same bright red dress, same hairdo. As soon as she let the bag fell on the floor and got into her black long robe, which she found still hanging behind the door, Pauper and the Aromatist entered carrying Olga's body. They placed it on the floor in the middle of the room where once their baba's corpse had lain and without exchanging any words they went outside. Kyra Vana, as if she was expecting her daughter, filled a long wooden tub with warm water, placed her inside and washed her with care. It was a liturgical, divine, gracious scene, as if she was giving a bath to a newborn. When she finished she placed Olga's body on the divan, dried it, dressed it in white, combed her hair and colored her lips bright red. Then she opened the canvas bag, which was filled with mauve wild flowers, and framed Olga's face.

On the day of her funeral, Olga looked more peaceful than she had ever looked.

"Look at her, she is exiting with joy," Kyra Vana said to Chrysa, who couldn't stop staring at the corpse.

"In the last few years she lived very happily, and that's because of you, Chrysa," added Fragile.

In fact Fragile's statement was 100 percent true. After many years of loneliness in America Olga finally had felt like part of a family, a new family, her brother's family, *the happiest family in the world*, as she used to say with pride.

Olga's death seemed natural, like a peaceful continuation. No one was surprised by her accident.

"By an accident you were conceived, by an accident you lived and by an accident you are going," Kyra Vana said when she kissed her daughter goodbye.

Olga was buried along with her nine mini bottles of Chanel No. 5.

"Even in heaven a bit of aroma is necessary," said Fragile, who couldn't stop her tears.

"And some love," added Chrysa, placing *The Faces of Love* between Olga's crossed hands. But the greatest goodbye gift of all was given to Olga by the Key-holder, who arrived only a few seconds before her body was covered in earth. That was a kiss; the first and last erotic kiss on Olga's lips sealed her brief life once and for all.

Common Era

The Beginning

Must I thus leave thee, Paradise?
—thus leave Thee, native soil,
these happy walks and shades?
John Milton, *Paradise Lost*, Book xi. Line 269

I was born on June 9, 1964, the last day of Paradise. Tuesday was the day but Sunday my parents named me. "In honor of your sweet little aunt who loved food more than life," my mama said in a low exhausted tone. She had suffered a lot.

"There were many complications," the doctor told my baba. "Complications that left your wife incapable of getting pregnant ever again."

My baba was relieved. *At least she won't have to go through all this pain ever again. At least all these nauseas, back pains, blue moods will never come back*, he thought to himself. *At least she is alive.*

The same night baba went to Paradise and bought ouzo shots for everybody.

"For my Chrysa," he said, raising his little glass into the air.

"And your daughter," yelled Dimitris.

"Yeah, yeah, for my daughter too, who got her baba's big eyes," added baba proudly.

The next day as my parents were bringing me home from the clinic, the Key-holder and Loo were taking down the Paradise's sign. By the time Olga welcomed my parents and myself into our new house, the new sign was up. It read in bright red letters:

LOO's

As my baba was staring at me the whole morning, Loo was staring at the new sign. He couldn't believe his eyes. For him owning a bar was more than serving cold beer and ouzo shots, it was a divine job, a godly service. "I will serve and serve and serve," he said looking at the sign proudly. "I will serve them all. As good as I can," he added at last with great determination.

He was very honored that his cousin had offered him the keys of Paradise and he had promised to do his best to keep it running smoothly.

"I will guard Paradise day and night," Loo said to his cousin months earlier.

"I know I know," mumbled the Key-holder, swallowing his tears. It was an emotional, touching scene for both men.

"You can always have it back," Loo said looking at his cousin's trembling hand.

"Nah, from now on SHE is yours and yours she'll remain," added the Key-holder, trying to resume his brave look. And a minute later, "One more thing, I want you to do one more thing for me."

"Whatever, just name it," replied Loo without hesitation.

"Rename her."

"Rename her?" repeated Loo in confusion.

"Yeah, rename her. It will be easier for me to let her go once you give her a new name."

"But Paradise is paradise. How on earth am I supposed to come up with a better name?" questioned Loo skeptically, dropping his head heavily between his hands.

"Paradise is paradise not because of the name," stated the Key-holder patting Loo's back.

Loo wasn't able to come up with a name. Nothing seemed to be good enough. Nothing seemed to match Paradise's paradisal persona. So after several months of waiting his cousin took the initiative. "I have a name for you," he told him, "it's simple and honest."

"Yeah? What is it?"

"Hand me a napkin," ordered the Key-holder without making eye contact.

Loo stretched his hand behind the bar, grabbed a couple of napkins and placed them on the bar counter.

"And that big red marker," the Key-holder ordered once again.

"Here you go," said Loo as he took off the marker, which was behind his ear.

The Key-holder unfolded one of the napkins, picked up the marker and wrote, "LOO's".

"Loo's?" asked Loo.

"Yeah. She is yours, right?" asked the Key-holder looking straight into Loo's eyes.

"I guess so," replied Loo with hesitation.

"There is nothing to guess. Here it is!" stated the Key-holder waving the napkin in front of Loo's face.

As much as Loo wanted Paradise, I wanted to be my baba's daughter. So the day I got my blood results, which was just a week after Maria's suicide attempt, I headed straight to Loo's. There I found Antonis. Alone. He offered a drink and I offered *an animal*. We started talking about this and that and wasted most of our breath on nonsense. Maria was at her house, George at his, Bo back in America. Fucking was one of those things that came up first and it was then that I admitted my sexual relation with Bo. I hadn't lied to Maria, she had just asked too early. Antonis knew nothing about Bo although he said that he had suspected it.

"Bo is too discrete. Doesn't share his fucking experiences, right?" I asked coolly.

"It's because it's fucking and not *jumping*," Antonis said, imitating Maria's sarcastic face and we both burst into laugher.

The truth was that I liked Antonis's remark 'cause I also liked to think that my relationship with Bo was more than simple *jumping*. Of course I wasn't sure if fucking was the right word but still *jumping* didn't justify what I felt that fall. In fact, the day that Bo was leaving for America I even believed for a second that I would be able to wait for him forever and ever. He might be the ONE! Thankfully I was wise enough to make no promises and neither did he. Later on when we exchanged letters we promised to have a *second round* as soon as he was back. Of course that never happened, although he was back several months later. It's better to have a friend than a second round, we both agreed when we met. So that was that.

After talking about fucking, Antonis and I talked about school, about Maria's parents, who were still unofficially divorced, and about Maria who was officially *a hurt, wounded kid*, as Loo put it when he heard about her suicide attempt. Then there was a full minute of silence. I felt that it was time to go on to the next thing, the thing that was troubling me the most, but I wasn't sure how to do it. So after a few moments of hesitation I handed Antonis the paper with my blood results. I couldn't put into words what was in that paper, so handing it to Antonis was the easiest way to handle the bad news. At first Antonis glanced at the paper without saying a word. For a sec I thought that he didn't want to have a part in any of that shit. Tired with my domestic bullshit, he was letting me swim in stinky caca without any intention to give me a hand. I was hurt but couldn't blame him. He had his own problems: his baba had died years ago and his mama was struggling to put bread on the table.

So I took the paper, thrust it into my pocket and said, "Well, shit happens."

"Nah, shit doesn't just happen," Antonis objected, looking straight into my eyes.

"Whatever," I mumbled lowering my gaze.

"No, shit does not just happen," he repeated once again in half the speed. "For one thing there is a connection between assholes and shit. You might even say that there is a positive correlation between these two; the more assholes the greater the shit and vice versa," he added seriously. Then he reached his hand into my pocket, pulled out the paper, and held it in front of my face, "So shit doesn't just happen, the assholes create the shit and not the other way around. Got it?" he asked, still holding the paper too close to my face.

"Got it," I said but really didn't understand what he meant.

"This is nothing like the chicken and the egg story," he went on and lit another cigarette. "This is pretty ancient shit and has nothing to do with you, so wipe it off and get on with your life. Anyway it's in your hands to decide what you want your future to look like. It's in your hands to make up your own fate," he said with confidence and started creating his prefect-shape smoke rings.

"Fate can't be made up," I said in a low, gloomy tone.

"Of course it can, faith can make up fate. Faith, nothing else," he replied putting his Camel between my lips.

For weeks I carried the piece of paper with my blood results in my right pocket. Squeezed it hard and harder. Even while I was sleeping my right hand was awake. I thought and thought and thought. I was angry and then angrier and one day I gave up on angrier 'cause I couldn't feel my right hand. And then I saw baba at our store. He came, signed up some papers, put them underneath the register, and as he was about to leave our eyes met. His gaze invited me to come closer to him. I won't move. I am not going anywhere near him, I thought and kept saying it in my head as my legs started to disobey me.

You are a fucking sissy, a fucking stupid gutless sissy, a voice yelled inside me as he was squeezing me in his arms a couple of minutes later. I said nothing to mama about this, but that day I didn't think about the piece of paper in my right pocket. In the afternoon, I went to Loo's to have my usual. Antonis was there. We talked and laughed and laughed and talked. As I was about to leave he asked, "What happened? Got rid of the shit?"

"Shit? What shit?" I replied and exited with a wink.

Once I arrived home, I went straight into my room. I took out my notebook and a pen and started writing. I wrote and wrote and wrote. For days I did almost nothing else. My pen flew over the paper and as the pages were getting heavy with words, I was getting lighter. There was an opening inside me and with each day that passed it was becoming bigger. One day it got so big that it felt as if I was nothing at all. That day baba got home. Faith transformed into fate, beliefs into facts and from one f word to the other, life returned to normal.

"You are lucky to get your family back," Maria remarked.

Her parents were the first to get officially divorced in our village.

"I knew it from the start," George stated with confidence.

"After all splits don't always happen," Bo added.

"Facts are facts," observed Wicked Yiayia proudly.

Books Available from Gival Press

A Change of Heart by David Garrett Izzo

1st edition, ISBN 1-928589-18-9, (ISBN 13: 978-1-928589-18-1), $20.00

A historical novel about Aldous Huxley and his circle "astonishingly alive and accurate."
— Roger Lathbury, George Mason University

An Interdisciplinary Introduction to Women's Studies Edited by Brianne Friel & Robert L. Giron

1ˢᵗ edition, ISBN 1-928589-29-4, (ISBN 13: 978-1-928589-29-7), $25.00

Winner of the 2005 DIY Book Festival Award for Compilations/ Anthologies.
A succinct collection of articles written for the college student of women's studies, covering a variety of disciplines from politics to philosophy.

Bones Washed With Wine: Flint Shards from Sussex and Bliss by Jeff Mann

1st edition, ISBN 1-928589-14-6, (ISBN 13: 978-1-928589-14-3), $15.00

A special collection of lyric intensity, including the 1999 Gival Press Poetry Award winning collection. Jeff Mann is "a poet to treasure both for the wealth of his language and the generosity of his spirit."— Edward Falco, author of *Acid*

Boys, Lost & Found: Stories by Charles Casillo

1ˢᵗ edition, ISBN 1-928559-33-2, (ISBN 13: 978-1-928589-33-4), $20.00

Casillo's boys are hustlers, writers, models, cruisers, lovers— complicated, smart, cool, witty, lusty, and romantic. "...fascinating, often funny... a safari through the perils and joys of gay life." —Edward Field

Canciones para sola cuerda / Songs for a Single String by Jesús Gardea; English translation by Robert L. Giron

1st edition, ISBN 1-928589-09-X, (ISBN 13: 978-1-928589-09-9), $15.00

Finalist for the 2003 Violet Crown Book Award for Literary Prose & Poetry.

A moving collection of love poems, with echoes of Neruda *à la Mexicana* as Gardea writes about the primeval quest for the perfect woman. "The free verse...evokes the quality and forms of *cante hondo*, emphasizing the emotional interplay of human voice and guitar."— Elizabeth Huergo, Montgomery College

Dead Time / Tiempo muerto by Carlos Rubio
1st edition, ISBN 1-928589-17-0, (ISBN 13: 978-1-928589-17-4), $21.00
Winner of the 2003 Silver Award for Translation—ForeWord Magazine's Book of the Year.
This bilingual (English/Spanish) novel is "an unusual tale of love, hate, passion and revenge." — Karen Sealy, author of *The Eighth House*

Dervish by Gerard Wozek
1st edition, ISBN 1-928589-11-1, (ISBN 13: 978-1-928589-11-2), $15.00
Winner of the 2000 Gival Press Poetry Award.
This rich whirl of the dervish traverses a grand expanse from bars to crazy dreams to fruition of desire. "By Jove, these poems shimmer."— Gerry Gomez Pearlberg, author of *Mr. Bluebird*

Dreams and Other Ailments / Sueños y otros achaques by Teresa Bevin
1st edition, ISBN 1-928589-13-8, (ISBN 13: 978-1-928589-13-6), $21.00
Winner of the 2001 Bronze Award for Translation—ForeWord Magazine's Book of the Year.
A wonderful array of short stories about the fantasy of life and tragedy but filled with humor and hope. "*Dreams and Other Ailments* will lift your spirits."— Lynne Greeley, The University of Vermont

The Gay Herman Melville Reader Edited by Ken Schellenberg
1st edition, ISBN 1-928589-19-7, (ISBN 13: 978-1-928589-19-8), $16.00
A superb selection of Melville's work. "Here in one anthology are the selections from which a serious argument can be made by both readers and scholars that a subtext exists that can be seen as homoerotic."— David Garrett Izzo, author of *Christopher Isherwood: His Era, His Gang, and the Legacy of the Truly Strong Man*

The Great Canopy by Paula Goldman

1st edition, ISBN 1-928589-31-6, (ISBN 13: 978-1-928589-31-0), $15.00

Winner of the 2004 Gival Press Poetry Award & Semi-Finalist for the 2006 Independent Publisher Book Award for Poetry.
"Under this canopy we experience the physicality of the body through Goldman's wonderfully muscular verse as well the analytics of a mind that tackles the meaning of Orpheus or the notion of desire."—Richard Jackson, author of *Half Lives, Heartwall,* and *Unauthorized Autobiography: New & Selected Poems*

The Last Day of Paradise by Kiki Denis

1st edition, ISBN 1-928589-32-4 (ISBN 13: 978-1-928589-32-7), $20.00

Winner of the 2005 Gival Press Novel Award.
"...Denis's debut is a slippery in-your-face accelerated rush of sex, hokum, and Greek family life. A little bit Eurydice, a little bit Chick-lit, with non-stop riffing on reality...."—Richard Peabody, editor of *Mondo Barbie*

Let Orpheus Take Your Hand by George Klawitter

1st edition, ISBN 1-928589-16-2, (ISBN 13: 978-1-928589-16-7), $15.00

Winner of the 2001 Gival Press Poetry Award.
A thought provoking work that mixes the spiritual with stealthy desire, with Orpheus leading us out of the pit. "These poems present deliciously sly metaphors of the erotic life that keep one reading on, and chuckling with pleasure."— Edward Field, author of *Stand Up, Friend, With Me*

Literatures of the African Diaspora by Yemi D. Ogunyemi

1st edition, ISBN 1-928589-22-7, (ISBN 13: 978-1-928589-22-8), $20.00

An important study of the influences in literatures of the world. "It, indeed, proves that African literatures are, without mincing words, a fountainhead of literary divergence."—Joshua 'Kunle Awosan, University of Massachusetts Dartmouth

Maximus in Catland by David Garrett Izzo

1st edition, ISBN 1-928589-34-0, (ISBN 13: 978-1-928589-34-1), $20.00

"… [an] examination of the idea of the Truly Strong Man—or, in this case, Cat—which is one who would give his own life for the sake of transpersonal good…This book is a treat—with a truly mystical message.—Toby Johnson, author of *Secret Matter*, winner of the Lambda Literary Award for Sci-Fi

Metamorphosis of the Serpent God by Robert L. Giron

1st edition, ISBN 1-928589-07-3, (ISBN 13: 978-1-928589-07-5), $12.00

"Robert Giron's biographical poetry embraces the past and the present, ethnic and sexual identity, themes both mythical and personal."— *The Midwest Book Review*

Middlebrow Annoyances: American Drama in the 21st Century by Myles Weber

1st edition, ISBN 1-928589-20-0, (ISBN 13: 978-1-928589-20-4), $20.00

"Weber's intelligence and integrity are unsurpassed by anyone writing about the American theatre today…"— John W. Crowley, The University of Alabama at Tuscaloosa

The Nature Sonnets by Jill Williams

1st edition, ISBN 1-928589-10-3, (ISBN 13: 978-1-928589-10-5), $8.95

An innovative collection of sonnets that speaks to the cycle of nature and life, crafted with wit and clarity. "Refreshing and pleasing."— Miles David Moore, author of *The Bears of Paris*

Poetic Voices Without Borders Edited by Robert L. Giron

1st edition, ISBN 1-928589-30-8, (ISBN 13: 978-1-928589-30-3), $20.00

Winner of the 2006 Writers Notes Book Award—Notable for Art & Semi-Finalist for the 2006 Independent Publisher Book Award for Anthologies.
"…This book is edgy with a literary inclusiveness…Each voice is unique, yet together they create oneness even as they individually represent societal diversity."—Lucinda Farrokh, LareDOS: A Journal of the Borderlands

On the Altar of Greece by Donna J. Gelagotis Lee
1ˢᵗ edition, ISBN 1-928589-36-7, (ISBN 13: 978-1-928589-35-5), $15.00

Winner of the 2005 Gival Press Poetry Award.
"...the journey of our time at this altar offers us a striking, immense set of views of a world we thought we knew, and still, wonderfully, do know in much richer ways by the end."—Don Berger, author of *Quality Hill* and *The Cream-Filled Muse*

On the Tongue by Jeff Mann
1ˢᵗ edition, ISBN 1-928589-35-9, (ISBN 13: 978-1-928589-35-8), $15.00

"...brilliantly pagan eroticism, at once tender, yet forceful and hard, like the hard-shelled seeds that spring from the fragilest of flowers. These poems are both, and in that breadth, nothing short of extraordinary..."—Trebor Healey, author of *Through It Came Bright Colors*

Prosody in England and Elsewhere: A Comparative Approach by Leonardo Malcovati
1st edition, ISBN 1-928589-26-X, (ISBN 13: 978-1-928589-26-6), $20.00

"To write about the structure of poetry for a non-specialist audience takes a brave author. To do so in a way that is readable, in fact enjoyable, without sacrificing scholarly standards takes an accomplished author."—Frank Anshen, State University of New York

Secret Memories / Recuerdos secretos by Carlos Rubio
1ˢᵗ edition, ISBN 1-928589-27-8, (ISBN 13: 978-1-928589-27-3), $21.00

Finalist for the 2005 ForeWord Magazine's Book of Year Award for Translation.
"From the beginning, the reader feels pulled into the narrator's world and observes, along with him, a delicate, beautiful, and vulnerable universe as personal and intimate as a conversation between lovers."
—Hope Maxell Snyder, author of *Orange Wine*

The Smoke Week: Sept. 11-21, 2001 by Ellis Avery

1st edition, ISBN 1-928589-24-3, (ISBN 13: 978-1-928589-24-2), $15.00

Winner of the 2004 Writer's Notes Magazine Book Award— Notable for Culture & Winner of the Ohioana Library Walter Rumsey Marvin Award.
"Here is Witness. Here is Testimony."— Maxine Hong Kingston, author of *The Fifth Book of Peace*

Songs for the Spirit by Robert L. Giron

1st edition, ISBN 1-928589-08-1, (ISBN 13: 978-1-928589-08-2), $16.95

This humanist collection invokes a new vision, one that speaks to readers regardless of their spiritual inclination. "This is an extraordinary book."— John Shelby Spong, author of *Why Christianity Must Change or Die: A Bishop Speaks to Believers in Exile*

Sweet to Burn by Beverly Burch

1st edition, ISBN 1-928589-23-5, (ISBN 13: 978-1-928589-23-5), $15.00

Winner of the 2004 Lambda Literary Award for Lesbian Poetry & Winner of the 2003 Gival Press Poetry Award.
"Novelistic in scope, but packing the emotional intensity of lyric poetry..."— Eloise Klein Healy, author of *Passing*

Tickets to a Closing Play by Janet I. Buck

1st edition, ISBN 1-928589-25-1, (ISBN 13: 978-1-928589-25-9), $15.00

Winner of the 2002 Gival Press Poetry Award.
"...this rich and vibrant collection of poetry [is] not only serious and insightful, but a sheer delight to read."— Jane Butkin Roth, editor, *We Used to Be Wives: Divorce Unveiled Through Poetry*

Wrestling with Wood by Robert L. Giron

3rd edition, ISBN 1-928589-05-7, (ISBN 13: 978-1-928589-05-1), $5.95

A chapbook of impressionist moods and feelings of a long-term relationship which ended in a tragic death. "Nuggets of truth and beauty sprout within our souls."— Teresa Bevin, author of *Havana Split*

Books for Children

Barnyard Buddies I by Pamela Brown; illustrations by Annie H. Hutchins
1st edition, ISBN 1-928589-15-4, (ISBN 13: 978-1-928589-15-0), $16.00

Thirteen stories filled with a cast of creative creatures both engaging and educational. "These stories in this series are delightful. They are wise little fables, and I found them fabulous."
—Robert Morgan, author of *This Rock* and *Gap Creek*

Barnyard Buddies II by Pamela Brown; illustrations by Annie H. Hutchins
1st edition, ISBN 1-928589-21-9, (ISBN 13: 978-1-928589-21-1), $16.00

"Children's literature which emphasizes good character development is a welcome addition to educators' as well as parents' resources."
—Susan McCravy, elementary school teacher

Tina Springs into Summer / Tina se lanza al verano by Teresa Bevin; illustrations by Perfecto Rodriguez
1ᵗ edition, ISBN 1-928589-28-6, (ISBN 13: 978-1-928589-28-0), $21.00

Winner of the 2006 Writer's Notes Magazine Book Award—Notable for Young Adult Literature.
"This appealing book with its illustrations can serve as a wonderful learning tool for children in grades 3-6. Bevin clearly understands the thoughts, feelings, and typical behaviors of pre-teen youngsters from multi-cultural urban backgrounds...."
—Dr. Nancy Boyd Webb, Professor of Social Work, author and editor, *Play Therapy for Children in Crisis* and *Mass Trauma and Violence*

Inquiries: 703.351.0079
Books available
via Ingram, the Internet, and other outlets.
Or Write:
Gival Press, LLC
PO Box 3812
Arlington, VA 22203
Visit: *www.givalpress.com*